Penelope Bailey
Takes the Stage

Susanna Reich

Marshall Cavendish

Marshall Cavendish Corporation
99 White Plains Road
Tarrytown, NY 10591
www.marshallcavendish.us

Library of Congress Cataloging-in-Publication Data
Reich, Susanna.
Penelope Bailey takes the stage / by Susanna Reich.
p. cm.
Summary: Against the wishes of her disapproving aunt, with whom she lives in 1889 San
Francisco while her parents are on a scientific expedition, eleven-year-old Penny tries to
prepare herself for an acting career.
ISBN-13: 978-0-7614-5287-4
ISBN-10: 0-7614-5287-7
[1. Sex role—Fiction. 2. Aunts—Fiction. 3. Theater—Fiction.
4. San Francisco (Calif.)—History—19th century—Fiction.] I. Title.
PZ7.R26343Pen 2006
[Fic]—dc22
2005020123

The text of this set book is set in Janson.
Book design by Symon Chow
Printed in The United States of America
First edition
10 9 8 7 6 5 4 3 2 1

ⅿℂ Marshall Cavendish

To Laurel Golio, daughter extraordinaire

Table of Contents

Chapter 1	Bad News	1
Chapter 2	Born to Be an Actress	5
Chapter 3	Farewells	9
Chapter 4	A Proper Family Dinner	15
Chapter 5	Pirates	21
Chapter 6	Plays Are for Girls	25
Chapter 7	The Dressmaker	29
Chapter 8	Punishment	37
Chapter 9	The Beach	43
Chapter 10	Miss Stipp	49
Chapter 11	"Oh Lonesome Soul"	59
Chapter 12	The Musicale	67
Chapter 13	The Party	73
Chapter 14	A Chance Encounter	81
Chapter 15	School	87
Chapter 16	A Grand Idea	97
Chapter 17	A Wish Comes True	103
Chapter 18	Isabelle in the Park	111
Chapter 19	*"The Play's the Thing"*	121
Chapter 20	The Kiss	127
Chapter 21	In the Garden	135
Chapter 22	Caught	141
Chapter 23	The Worst Thing That Could Happen	145
Chapter 24	The Escape	149
Chapter 25	Searching for Isabelle	155
Chapter 26	The Dance	161
Chapter 27	The Unexpected Guest	171
Chapter 28	The Homecoming	177
Chapter 29	Petunia's Request	183
Chapter 30	The Switch	187
Chapter 31	*"All's Well That Ends Well"*	193
	Author's Note	
	A Note About Sources	

"All the world's a stage"

from *As You Like It*,
by William Shakespeare

CHAPTER ONE

Bad News

Mama was scrubbing potatoes at the kitchen sink when I burst through the door. I tossed my rucksack in the direction of a chair, hiked up my skirts, and began to unhook my shoes.

"No more pencils, no more books, no more teachers—"

"Penny!" said Mama, laughing. "You are a whirlwind!" She pushed a wisp of hair out of her eyes with the back of her dripping hand. "How was your last day of school?"

I unhooked a stubborn button and yanked off my shoes. Hurrah! No more cooped-up feet! My toes wriggled with happiness.

"Miss Barker says next year Cassie and I can recite scenes from Shakespeare, and I'm going to practice my elocution over the summer so everyone will understand me when I get up on stage, and Cassie said her mother would get some old velvet drapes and sew costumes for us, and—do you think I'd look good as Juliet? A skinny Juliet with red hair?—and Cassie'll be Romeo, and we're going to practice over the summer so as soon as school starts we can show Miss Barker, and we're going to be splendid!"

I hopped from one foot to the other.

"We'll see, sweetheart," said Mama. She dug a brown spot out of a potato, then put down her knife. "Sit down, dear. I must talk to you about something."

I was too excited to sit. I danced around the table until Mama put a hand on my arm.

"Penny. Calm down. It's hot."

I hadn't noticed. I wiped my neck. It felt gritty. I looked down and saw that my pinafore was covered with dust from the road.

"Sorry," I said, collapsing into a chair.

Mama wiped her hands on her apron and sat down, too.

"Now Penny," she said, "you might not like what I'm about to say, but I want you to listen carefully. You know that Papa is supposed to be home by the end of the summer, don't you?"

I nodded.

"Well, today I received a letter from him. His department at the university has agreed to extend his trip for one more semester. He wants to complete his research on the butterfly species he's been studying. I'm afraid he won't be home till December."

"December! That's six more months!"

"Yes."

"That's rotten!"

She raised her eyebrows.

"It's not very nice of him," I said.

"Now, Penny—"

"He likes those dead butterflies," I said. "You'd think someone smart enough to be a professor at the University of California at Berkeley would be able to pay more attention to his only—"

"Penny—" Mama said with a warning tone.

I sighed. "Well," I said. "I suppose it can't be helped." I stood up. "May I go outside?"

"No dear," she said. "Not yet." She took my hand in hers.

The look on her face filled me with alarm. "What's the matter? Is Papa ill?"

"No. It's his assistant, Mr. Phroups. He's broken his leg."

I barely knew Mr. Phroups, but still I felt sorry for him. "Will he be all right?"

"Yes. Papa says the leg swelled up, but the doctor applied compresses. It's a clean break. The doctor set the leg, and Mr. Phroups is resting. He's to sail home on the next boat."

"I'm glad Papa's all right," I said, relieved. "Now may I go outside?"

"Penny, listen," said Mama. "Papa has an enormous amount of work to do. With Mr. Phroups gone, he has no one to help him. They've been in the field for months, not only collecting butterflies but also plants for the Botany Department, and without Mr. Phroups to help identify and sketch them, Papa will never be able to finish in time."

"Oh," I said. I glanced at the door.

She sighed. "I don't quite know how to say this. Your father and I . . . Papa feels that I'm the only person who knows enough about his research to take over for Mr. Phroups. With my drawing experience I can be especially helpful with the plants. So Papa has asked me to come—"

"We're going to join Papa on his expedition?" I shouted, leaping to my feet.

"No, dear. *I'm* going to join Papa in the islands, and you're staying here."

"Staying here! Why?"

"I'm to depart in one week."

"One week! But why can't I come?"

"I'll be busy helping Papa."

"That's a foolish reason! Why can't I help? I want to see Papa! I can draw. I'm a good drawer. You said so yourself. You said I was an artist, like you."

"You're a very good drawer, dear, and you're a wonderful help, but you'll be safer here. There are dangerous tropical diseases there."

"I'm healthy!"

"I know you're healthy. Hawaii is simply not a wholesome

environment for an eleven-year-old girl."

"Eleven and a half!"

"Now, Penny. I've given this a great deal of thought. You know Aunt Phyllis and Uncle Henry have always said you could stay with them if we had to go on an expedition."

"Aunt Phyllis?"

"I've written to Aunt Phyllis, and it's all arranged. You'll spend the summer with your cousins across the bay in San Francisco. And go to school with them in the fall."

"Aunt Phyllis . . . go to school . . . with *them*? What about Shakespeare? What about Cassie? What about *Romeo and Juliet*? I won't go. I WON'T! How could you make me live with that awful woman and her awful daughters?"

"Look, I know Phyllis is a bit stiff, but she's your aunt. She'll take good care of you. As for the girls, perhaps Violet has become a little more mature, now that she's nearly fourteen. And you mustn't mind Petunia. She's younger than you by two years. You mustn't be so sensitive to her slights. Besides, you and Cousin Aldy get along fine, and though he's a boy, he's the same age as you, and I—"

I didn't wait for her to finish. I ran from the kitchen and out the back door. I ran straight to my secret spot behind the bushes and threw myself on the grass.

CHAPTER TWO

~~~

Born to Be an Actress

Go without me? I punched the grass with my fist and sobbed. *How could they do such a thing? Cassie and I were going to have a perfect summer, right here in Berkeley. We were going to practice* Romeo and Juliet *and tell secrets and explore in the attic. We were going to pack picnic lunches and have expeditions up Strawberry Canyon and play with Cassie's dog Matilda—and oh! Now I won't be able to see Matilda's puppies being born!*

I was so angry I cried a river of tears. A great big river, wider than the Mississippi. I wished that river would drown the whole yard and the house and everything in it. Even Mama.

After a while the tears slowed, and I turned to face the sky. I lay there for a long time, watching the clouds. Finally I sat up and dried my face. My hands were filthy. I wiped them on my pinafore.

At this rate I'll never become an actress, and Papa will never pay more attention to me. I hate his stupid butterflies. I hate Aunt Phyllis. And her house, too. So dark and dreary, and with so many rules!

I won't let it happen.

The very next day Mama went up to the attic and brought down the steamer trunks. Those trunks had been gathering dust in the attic for seven years—ever since we rode the transcontinental railroad from Cambridge, Massachusetts, in 1882.

When I saw the trunks I locked myself in my room. Mama didn't say a word. By the end of the day, I was so hungry I came out. At supper I was sullen. Mama had made pot roast, my favorite. I ate some meat, but I did *not* eat any vegetables.

The next day I had to help pack. I pouted and fumed, but Mama didn't scold me, not once.

All week we packed and packed and packed. Mama made me throw sheets over the furniture, and empty the larder, and give the canary and the potted ferns to Mrs. Harper, our neighbor. We rolled up Mama's canvases and put away her brushes and packed up her drawing paper, pencils, and charcoal. When we closed up Mama's painting studio, she seemed terribly sad. I didn't give up hope. Maybe she'd change her mind.

On the last day Mama sent me down the street to Cassie's to say good-bye. Cassie and I hugged each other and promised to write faithfully. Matilda wagged her tail and rolled over on the floor. I patted her furry belly and hugged Cassie again. Mrs. Blake, Cassie's mother, had to pry us apart.

That night Mama called me into her bedroom one last time to do our beauty exercises. We were dressed in our nightclothes, as usual, and Mama's hair was set with crimping pins. She held on to the bedpost, and I held on to the chair.

"Rise, rise, to the tips of your toes, reach up to heaven as far as it goes," she said.

But I didn't much feel like reaching.

"Plunge, plunge, to the depths of the sea, fall to the floor and rise to your knee," she said.

But I didn't much feel like plunging.

Out the window I could see the fog rolling in from the ocean. It swallowed San Francisco and Mount Tamalpais and curled its way across San Francisco Bay toward Berkeley.

Let it swallow Aunt Phyllis and never spit her up.

I looked at Mama. She was standing on one leg and swinging the other up and down. My legs felt like they were filled with bricks. Mama stopped swinging her leg.

"Why don't we turn in now, sweetie," she said.

She put her arm around me and walked me to my room. I climbed into bed while Mama drew the curtains shut.

"Who will tuck me in at Aunt Phyllis's house?"

"Aunt Phyllis will, of course," said Mama. She kissed me on the forehead and placed Miranda, my doll, in my arms. "And Miranda will keep you company." She started to leave.

"Stay, Mama."

She sat on the edge of the bed.

"Are you sure I can't go to the islands with you?"

She pulled a handkerchief out of her sleeve. "No, dear. We've already discussed that. Go to sleep now."

We were quiet for a while, and then I said, "Could you please open the window?"

Through the open window I could smell eucalyptus trees. I loved that smell.

"I can draw plants, too," I said.

"You do draw very well, dear," said Mama, wiping her eyes.

"What if something happens to your ship? I thought you were afraid of the ocean."

She looked out the window. "I'm doing this for Papa. He needs me. Sometimes one must put one's fears aside."

A breeze ruffled the white muslin curtain.

"I need you, too," I said.

"Oh, Penny. Do you think this is easy for me?" She wiped her eyes again.

"Don't cry," I said.

She patted my hand.

"Mama? If I promise to be a good girl, will you let me take elocution lessons when you return? So I can practice my pronunciation for when I become an actress? Please?" I had wanted to be an actress ever since Papa had taken me to see a performance of *A Midsummer Night's Dream* at the university when I was eight.

She smiled. "You do have a notion to become an actress, don't you? All right. I see how much it means to you. But you must keep your promise and obey Aunt Phyllis."

"I will!" I said. "Do you think they'll let me recite Shakespeare in the San Francisco school?"

"Penny, you know Papa and I enjoy the theater, but Aunt Phyllis is . . . well, she's rather old-fashioned. I don't think she'd send her children to a school where acting is encouraged."

"But Shakespeare! Everyone knows Shakespeare is—"

"Hush, now. Let's go to sleep."

"Perhaps you could speak to Aunt Phyllis. I'm almost twelve, and if I'm going to be an actress—"

"Penny, your dream is very sweet, but I'm sure Aunt Phyllis believes that proper young ladies do not become actresses. That will have to wait until we come back. Now it's time to be quiet."

"But I can't wait. And it's not a dream. It's my *destiny*."

Mama smiled. "We'll see."

"I was born to be an actress."

"Shhh," she whispered. "Good night."

I rolled onto my side and curled myself around Miranda.

Six months of Aunt Phyllis and her insufferable rules! I don't care what anybody thinks. No one—not even Aunt Phyllis—is going to keep me off the stage.

CHAPTER THREE

Farewells

The morning of our departure for San Francisco dawned cool and foggy. We rose early, as Mama said we had to tidy up some loose ends before we took the horse and buggy down to the steamer ferry in Oakland. We ate what was left in the pantry, put away every last little thing, closed all the drapes, and locked the house. By the time the horse and buggy arrived, it was noon. The driver carried the trunks to the waiting carriage. I took one last look around.

Good-bye, house. Good-bye, swing. Good-bye, hiding place.

I found a eucalyptus leaf on the ground and slipped it into the pocket of my sweater. As the carriage pulled away, I held my breath, and when I looked back at our brown shingled house with its shutters closed up tight, it looked like the house wasn't breathing either.

Mama bought two ferry tickets, fifteen cents each. I could tell she was a bit nervous because she kept rearranging our luggage. Mama doesn't like boats. She's afraid of the water because she can't swim.

We boarded the ferry and crossed the wide bay. Mama held my hand. San Francisco looked very small and far away when we started out, but as we got closer it got bigger and bigger. The waves on the bay were high, and I felt a little seasick as I watched the foam appear and disappear from the tops of the waves. Seagulls swirled about the boat, diving for fish in the choppy water. The air smelled salty. It pricked my nose.

At the pier we hailed a hackney with a sorry-looking swayback horse to take us to Aunt Phyllis and Uncle Henry's house. The driver put our trunks on top of the carriage. Up and down the steep hills of San Francisco we made our way. The horse plodded along, which was fine with me. I was in no hurry to get there. I huddled close to Mama. Her boat was set to sail that very evening.

When the carriage pulled up to the gray wooden house on Franklin Street, I was struck by how big it was. I supposed it had to be big to hold a family with three children, two servants, and a father who stands over six feet high and works in the China trade. But as grand as the house looked, I still wondered: *Would there truly be room for me?*

Mama knocked on the black door with the brass dragon knocker. A minute later the door swung open. Aunt Phyllis loomed before us in a bright blue dress with an enormous bustle. She looked like a peacock.

"My, my, Penelope, you don't look well at all," she said, pulling me inside. She grabbed my face and turned it up so she could get a good look at me. Then she pecked me on the head with a kiss.

"What took you so long?" she asked Mama.

Mama murmured something about how the ferry had had a hard time docking on account of the high swells in the bay, but Aunt Phyllis waved Mama's words away.

"You don't have much time," Aunt Phyllis said.

The carriage driver was struggling up the front steps with my trunk on his back. He set it down for a minute to consider how to fit it through the door. The poor man was perspiring so much, he looked like someone had dumped a pail of water on his head.

"Upstairs," said Aunt Phyllis, with a flick of her wrist.

The man was taller than Aunt Phyllis, but she seemed to look down upon him nonetheless.

"Second bedroom on the left," she said. "You may wait in the cab for Mrs. Bailey. She departs for the wharf in half an hour."

"Yes, ma'am," the man said. He glanced at Mama and raised his eyebrows.

Mama raised her eyebrows, too, but all she said was, "Penny, why don't you go up and say hello to your cousins while Aunt Phyllis and I settle a few details?"

I didn't want to say hello to my cousins. I wanted to spend every last second with Mama. I grabbed her hand.

"You may go upstairs now, Penelope," said Aunt Phyllis.

I looked at Mama, but she just nodded, so I made my way up the stairs. The hall was dark and gloomy. Several large mahogany cabinets stood against the walls, separated here and there by small, uncomfortable-looking black lacquered chairs with cane seats. Blue and white Chinese plates were lined up in rows inside the cabinets, and there were pictures on the walls in fancy gold frames. Some were portraits of Aunt Phyllis's serious-looking relatives, but there were also a few pictures from China. I stopped to look at a particularly lovely one of a man pushing a boat down a river with a big pole. The boat made ripples in the water. Over in the corner of the picture, flowering branches were bending low.

Violet's door was open. I peeked in, but nobody was there. I walked down the hall to Petunia's room. The door was shut.

"Hello? Petunia?" I called.

There was no answer, so I opened the door. Petunia was sitting on the bed, reading a book. She didn't look up, and she didn't say hello.

"Hello," I said again.

Not taking her eyes off her book, she nodded, just enough to set her brown ringlets bobbing. I backed out the door.

Where's Aldy? I wondered.

I checked his room, but it was empty. Perhaps he was outside. I wandered down the back stairs. As I stepped into the kitchen, Aldy almost knocked me over.

"Penny!" he cried, stuffing the remains of a roll into his mouth. "I've been waiting for you all day!"

His shirttails were hanging out of his pants, and his curly, blond hair was pasted to his pink forehead. He grabbed my arm and yanked me out the back door.

In the corner of the yard I spied a pile of wood. Someone had painted a skull and crossbones on one of the planks.

"Is this a pirate ship?"

"Yes, and I'm captain," said Aldy.

I circled the pile. Ideas were popping in my head. "This could be the gangplank, and here's the captain's quarters, and this is the crow's nest."

"And this is the galley," he added. "Where we eat."

"Let's make up a play about pirates," I said.

"Okay. You're assistant captain. I mean first mate."

I was about to board the ship when Aunt Phyllis appeared at the kitchen door.

"Penelope, it's time to say good-bye to your mother."

I climbed down and followed Aunt Phyllis into the house. Mama was waiting in the front hall. Uncle Henry was there, too. He smiled his big smile, and I gave him a hug and a kiss. His mustache tickled my cheek.

Violet had appeared out of nowhere. She had filled out since the last time I saw her, but she hadn't turned up her hair yet. She was taller, too, almost as tall as Mama.

"Violet, say hello to your cousin," said Aunt Phyllis.

"Hullo," she mumbled. Peering into a mirror, she fluffed her curls.

Petunia tripped down the stairs, still reading her book.

Violet perked up. "Tuney, come here," she said. "You have to help me with my embroidery."

Petunia looked annoyed but said nothing. She closed her book and marched past me, her nose in the air. For a fourth grader, she sure had a trunkload of snobbery.

As the grownups chattered away, I glanced into the parlor. Petunia and Violet plumped their skirts and settled themselves on the fringed sofa like two prize chickens. They were acting like they were minding their own business, but I knew they were only there to spy on me. I could tell by the way they were straining their necks to see what was going on in the hall.

Aunt Phyllis had decided we wouldn't go down to the pier to see Mama off. She said she didn't like the sort of people who frequented that part of town. We had to make our farewells right there in the hall.

I clung to Mama's hand and stared at the floor. The afternoon sun was streaming through a stained-glass window on the landing halfway up the stairs. It cast a little beam of rose-colored light onto my shoes.

"You'll be a good girl now, won't you, Penny?" said Mama.

There was such a big lump in my throat, I couldn't say anything.

"Please don't give Aunt Phyllis and Uncle Henry any trouble," she added. Then she bent down and whispered in my ear so that only I could hear. "You'll remember your promise, sweetheart? Be a proper little lady?"

She put her arms around me. I hugged her tight. Her chest trembled ever so slightly. She wriggled free and straightened her coat, then wiped her eyes with her lace handkerchief. I looked away. She said we'd be together for Christmas and reminded me again not to give Aunt Phyllis and Uncle Henry any trouble.

I could feel Aunt Phyllis staring at me. She was standing with her arms across her chest, and for a moment she scowled at me.

Then she rearranged her face and smiled at Mama. I knew she couldn't wait to get her hands on me. I could tell she was planning to turn me into a prize chicken, just like Violet and Petunia.

Uncle Henry stood between the hat stand and the grandfather clock. "We'll have some fun this summer, eh?" he said, winking.

"Henry, please," said Aunt Phyllis.

I smiled. Uncle Henry liked to have fun, but Aunt Phyllis did her best to stop him.

Mama kept saying, "Thank you, Phyllis, Henry, thank you. I don't know what we'd do without you."

Aunt Phyllis just nodded and kept her thin little lips pressed tight together. Then Mama embraced Aunt Phyllis and Uncle Henry, and before you could say "abracadabra," the big, black door with the brass dragon knocker closed behind her, and she was gone.

CHAPTER FOUR

A Proper Family Dinner

"Come along, Penelope, it's time to dress for dinner," said Aunt Phyllis, sweeping herself and her bustle across the hall. "Violet, fetch your brother. Petunia, be a dear and show Penelope to her room. Dinner will be served promptly at six."

I trudged up the stairs behind Petunia. At the second bedroom on the left, she stopped.

"In here," she said, pointing.

I hesitated for a moment. Petunia pushed past me and went in. I peeked through the door. I had never been in the spare bedroom before. It was a large room with faded wallpaper and a high ceiling. An enormous four-poster bed with a lace bedspread was set against the far wall. Next to it stood a bedside table and a basket of dried-up roses. Against the right wall was an oak bureau with a mirror in a gilded frame. On the left, a large wardrobe for clothes reached to the ceiling. A Persian rug covered most of the floor.

My room at home was yellow, like sunshine. It was cheerful and happy. This room smelled like a musty attic. It seemed as if it hadn't been used in years.

Petunia sat on the trunk at the foot of the bed, one hand on the clasp.

"I suppose you're staying," she said.

I shrugged. "I suppose."

"Did you get seasick crossing the bay?"

"No," I lied. "Of course not."

"Not a particle?"

She seemed disappointed. I waited for her to say something else, but she merely sat and stared at me. Then she shrugged, stood, and started to open the trunk.

"Don't look in there," I said.

"Why not?"

"Because it's private, that's why not."

"Oh look, a little purse," she said.

"Put that back!" I said.

"I'm just trying to be friendly," she snapped. "There's probably no decent clothes in your stupid trunk anyway." She stomped out of the room.

I sank onto the trunk.

I hate you, Mama.

I hate you, Papa.

How could you do this to me?

The room was so stuffy, I thought I would suffocate. Two big windows faced the street, and there was a small window to the right of the bureau. I opened the small window, and the smell of the ocean flew into my face. I took a deep breath.

I walked over to the trunk and looked inside. Mama had left a little silk purse for me, as a surprise. In it was a dollar bill and a note.

Just in case, said the note.

A dollar bill! I was rich! I tucked the bill into the purse and placed it on the bedside table. What other treasures had Mama packed for me?

With a thrill I saw that she had tucked her paisley shawl under my clothing. I picked it up and wrapped it around me. How I loved this shawl, with its swirls of red and yellow and its touch of blue. Grandma Bailey had brought it all the way from Scotland. I held it to my cheek. It smelled like Mama. I pulled the shawl tight around my shoulders.

Catching sight of myself in the mirror, I imagined myself as Shakespeare's Juliet, leaning on her balcony, waiting for Romeo to appear.

"*O Romeo, Romeo! wherefore art thou, Romeo?*" I said to my imaginary audience.

Just then Aldy poked his head through the door.

"Didn't you hear the dinner bell? Mother will be angry if we're late!"

I threw down the shawl. It wouldn't do to cross Aunt Phyllis, not on my first day here. She was sour enough already.

What would Aunt Phyllis consider proper for dinner? I peeled off my travel clothes and slipped on a yellow cotton dress with white piping. There was no time to change into my fancy shoes. Better to wear my sturdy, brown ones than to risk being late for dinner.

As I stepped into the hall, Violet came out of her room. She had on an ice blue dress that exactly matched her eyes. I froze. She looked me up and down. Her gaze settled at my feet.

"Lovely shoes," she said, with a curl of her lip.

"Thank you," I said. Then, doing my best to ignore her, I turned and slowly descended the stairs.

Aunt Phyllis, Uncle Henry, Petunia, and Aldy were already seated at the dining room table, Uncle Henry at the head and Aunt Phyllis opposite him. They were all sitting bolt upright on the edge of their seats, except for Aldy. He was bouncing up and down.

"You may sit here, Penelope," said Aunt Phyllis, nodding in the direction of the chair next to her.

As Violet sat down she made a great show of flipping her hair over her shoulder.

"Violet, stop fussing," said Aunt Phyllis.

We bowed our heads while Aunt Phyllis said grace. Then she rang a little bell. The door to the kitchen swung open, and a servant girl appeared. I had never seen her before, so I supposed she must be new. She was wearing a gray uniform, and her hair was pulled back in a funny, little bun. Atop her head was perched a small, round hat.

She placed a tray with a porcelain soup tureen, six bowls, and a silver ladle on the sideboard. She ladled soup into the bowls and began to serve.

We waited for Aunt Phyllis to begin. Aldy started to make funny faces. I giggled. He rolled his eyes, and I laughed harder. Uncle Henry's eyes darted in my direction. A tiny smile flickered across his lips.

Aunt Phyllis turned to me. "What is so amusing, Penelope?" she said. "Aldebaran?"

She said his name Al-DEH-bah-ron. Like the star.

Aldy composed his face. "Nothing, Mother," he said.

"Hrumph," she said. "Young ladies should not call attention to themselves at the dinner table." She turned to Uncle Henry and picked up her spoon.

This was the sign we had been waiting for. We all picked up our spoons and started to eat. Zounds! I was beginning to starve to death right there at the dining table.

The rest of the meal proceeded without incident—salad course, fish course, sherbet, meat course, cheese course. Uncle Henry ate a lot, as did Aldy. Aunt Phyllis and the girls just picked at their food.

Uncle Henry talked about Chinese trade rules, and Aunt Phyllis talked about who had left calling cards that afternoon and which important people would be attending the hospital charity dinner. Nobody mentioned Mama or the long voyage that lay ahead of her. We children were not allowed to talk.

By the time dessert was served, my stomach was so full I thought I would burst. I was sorry to be so stuffed, as dessert was strawberry shortcake.

After the dishes were cleared, Aunt Phyllis and Uncle Henry kept talking. I looked out the window to see if there was any daylight left.

Finally Aunt Phyllis said, "Children, you may be excused."

Aldy and I looked at each other and raced for the kitchen door.

"Walk," said Aunt Phyllis.

We walked until we were safely in the kitchen, then ran for the back door.

CHAPTER FIVE

Pirates

"First one to the pirate ship gets to be captain!" yelled Aldy as he dashed out the door.

I lifted my skirts to run faster, but he got there first, despite his full belly.

"I'm captain!" he announced.

"I'm first mate!"

Aldy grabbed a stick and waved it in the air like a sword. "All right," he commanded, "these are your orders. Climb the mast and look for ships. If you see any, yell, 'Victims ahoy!'"

I hitched up my skirts and climbed the planks. The view was a fine one. I could see up the hill and down, and right into the neighbors' yards. The houses on Aldy's street were fancy, but they were set close together.

Right next door I spied a silver-haired gentleman and a lady, sipping coffee on a brick terrace.

"Victims, ahoy!" I said.

"Where?" said Aldy.

I pointed to the people next door.

Aldy climbed up. "They're not victims," he said. "They're Mr. and Mrs. Prenderwinkel. Our new neighbors. Mother doesn't like them."

"Why not?"

"They're actors."

"*Actors?*"

"Um-hm."

"Genuine professional actors, in a theater?"

"I suppose."

"You *suppose?* Have you ever spoken to them? Have you seen them act? What kind of plays are they in? Do you think we could go see them in a play?"

Aldy blinked at me. "No. I mean yes. I mean no. I only know they're actors because Mother said so. She says it's scandalous that people like *that* moved in next door."

"People like what?"

"*Actors,*" he said, pursing his lips in a perfect imitation of Aunt Phyllis.

We both laughed.

"I wish I knew some real actors," I said. "I'd like to meet this Mr. and Mrs. Prenderwinkel." I felt a burst of energy.

"Look! Here comes a victim now!" said Aldy, pointing to the kitchen door.

Mrs. Campbell, the cook, was standing on the back steps, shaking crumbs out of the white linen napkins we had used for dinner.

"Follow me," Aldy whispered, climbing down from the pirate ship.

We crept across the yard toward Mrs. Campbell, hiding behind bushes as we went. She was so busy shaking out the napkins she didn't see us. When she was finished, she scooped up the pile and turned to go into the house.

"Now!" whispered Aldy.

He leapt onto the steps, banging his stick on the banister.

"Your money or your life!" he cried.

"Give us your jewels or walk the gangplank!" I yelled.

Mrs. Campbell screamed and threw up her hands. Napkins scattered over the steps.

"Oh me lord! Ha' mercy!"

Then she saw it was us.

"Now will ya look and see what ya've made me do, Master Aldebaran! Yer Mum'll have me to her study if she finds dirt on the napkins. And you, missy! Ya ought ta know better, a young lady like yerself. Ya gave me quite a fright, jumpin' out like that."

She grabbed the banister to steady herself.

"I'm a goin' to tell yer mother right now, I am," she said to Aldy, scowling. "'Tis unbecomin' behavior fer a young lady," she added.

"Oh, Cook," said Aldy, "don't be angry. We were only playing."

"Playin'?" said Mrs. Campbell. "With pirates? And with Miss Penelope's mother sailin' out this evenin'? Did ya give no mind to the threat o' pirates for her and her ship? A whole month on the high seas?"

My mouth dropped open.

"That's right, Miss. You should be up in yer room prayin' for yer dear mother's soul, not out pretendin' to be a pirate. I've heard there's plenty o' pirates in those South Seas waters. Not to mention storms and hurry-canes and ty-poons!"

She turned on her heel and stomped back into the kitchen.

I stared after her.

"Aw, Penny, don't pay any attention to Cook," Aldy said. "She doesn't know what she's talking about."

But it was too late. Mrs. Campbell had put the thought of South Seas pirates into my head, and it wasn't coming out any time soon.

I shuddered and sat down on the steps.

"Do you think there are pirates in the South Seas?" I said.

"Of course not," said Aldy. But he didn't sound so sure.

"And now we're in trouble with Aunt Phyllis," I said.

"Naw," said Aldy. "Cook always says she's going to tell Mother, but she never does."

"She doesn't?"

"Not usually," said Aldy.

Just then Violet appeared at the French doors that opened into the backyard from Uncle Henry's study. "Aldebaran. Penelope. Mother says you're to come inside. Right now."

CHAPTER SIX

Plays Are for Girls

I looked at Aldy. He shrugged. We followed Violet into the house. Aunt Phyllis was sitting in the study. Twilight had fallen, and the gaslights had been lit. I walked right up to my aunt.

"We didn't mean any harm," I said. "We were only play-acting."

"Whatever are you mumbling about, child? It's getting late. To bed with you. There will be no playing outside in the dark."

Mrs. Campbell hadn't told her! I looked at Aldy. He smiled.

"Good night, Mother," he said.

"Good night," said Aunt Phyllis.

"Good night," I said.

Is that all? I thought.

Aldy and I climbed the stairs.

"Doesn't anybody tuck you in?" I asked.

"Not anymore. Mother thinks I'm too old. She says that's for babies."

I didn't say anything. I didn't want Aldy to think I was a baby. He turned in to his room.

"Aldy," I said. "Do you think I could meet your neighbors? The actors? Could you introduce us?"

"The Prenderwinkels aren't home very often."

"I bet they're at the theater all the time, rehearsing. Or on tour! Will you let me know if you see them?"

"Okay."

"And Aldy, do you want to do a play with me this summer? I'll make it up, and we'll get some of your friends for the other parts, and we can put it on for the parents."

His hand rested on the doorknob for a moment. Then he shook his head. "Nah. Plays are for girls. G'night." He shut his bedroom door behind him.

With a pang of disappointment I went into my room. Someone had turned on the gaslight next to the bed. It threw a feeble light across the floor. Reaching into the trunk, I found my flannel nightdress, my doll, Miranda, and my book of Shakespeare plays. I pulled out a pencil and paper, too, so I could write a letter to Mama.

San Francisco, July 2, 1889

Dear Mama,

I know your only gone a few hours but I had to write. You said its good to get things off your chest. No one tucked me in. ~~Aunt Phyllis is not very nice~~.

I wish I had seen your sailing ship. Is it big? Is it pretty when the wind fills the sails? Do the sailors climb all the way to the top of the masts? Did you make a drawing of them? I hope you are safe.

I know you probly will not get this letter for a few weeks and by then you will already be landed in the Sandwich islands. (That is what Miss Barker says they used to call Hawaii.) Please, please write as soon as you can. I miss you allready. <u>Please</u> say hello to Papa for me and give him <u>a big hug and a kiss</u>. Tell him I am practicing my Shakespeare so that I can be a famous actress when I grow up.

Your loving daugter,

Penelope

P.S. Do you think there are pirates in the South Seas?
P.P.S. What's a ty-poon?

I tucked the letter inside my Shakespeare book, where no one would see. Tomorrow I would get some stamps and post it.

The night air was chilly and damp. I shut the window and spread Mama's shawl over the bed. I turned down the gas, and the lamp sputtered out. The room was very dark, and it was very quiet, too, save for the occasional clip-clop of horses' hooves on the cobblestones below.

I curled up in bed and pulled Miranda close. As I fell asleep I thought of Mama all alone on the wide, wide ocean, and I wondered what dreadful things Aunt Phyllis had in store for me.

CHAPTER SEVEN

The Dressmaker

"Aldy. Psst."

"Unh. Go away."

"Get up, sleepyhead. It's morning. There's pirates in the backyard."

That made him sit up quick.

"C'mon," I said. "I want to look for your neighbors. The actors. What's their name?"

"Prenderwinkel," he said. "I have to dress first. Throw me my knickers."

"Right. Prenderwinkel. Can I watch you dress?"

"No! You wait outside."

"I was only fooling," I said, hitting him with a pillow.

He hit me back with another pillow, and before you could say "abracadabra," there were feathers flying everywhere.

By the end of the pillow fight, we were both lying on the floor. Suddenly the door popped open.

"Is this how young ladies start their day in Berkeley?"

I jumped up and straightened my clothes. "No! I mean, good morning, Aunt Phyllis, we didn't . . . That is, we were going to—"

"Pick up those pillows! Make yourself presentable and come down for breakfast. We have a busy day ahead of us. I have an

29

appointment with the dressmaker, and we have preparations to make for our Independence Day picnic tomorrow. I will see you downstairs in fifteen minutes."

With a sweep of her skirt she turned and left the room. A smell of soap hung in the air.

"I suppose we should clean up," I said, stooping to retrieve an escaped feather.

"I s'pose," said Aldy.

"Do you always have a July 4th picnic?" I said, picking up the pillows.

"Not always. Depends on the weather. Sometimes we go to the beach. If Father can convince Mother."

"The beach!" I said. "That's wonderful!"

He nodded.

"Completely marvelous!" I said, leaping onto the bed.

"Yup."

"Fantastically magnificently excellent!"

"Uh-huh."

"Then what are we waiting for?" I cried. "The sooner we get done with today, the sooner tomorrow will come!" And with that, I leapt off the bed, dashed from the room, and flew down the stairs to breakfast.

Breakfast was a help-yourself affair. On the sideboard there was some cold, lumpy-looking porridge, a bowl of stewed prunes, a plate of dried-up-looking toast, and a pot of tea. I poured some tea and nibbled on a piece of toast while I gazed at a painting that hung on the wall above the sideboard. It was a portrait of a young woman with sparkling eyes and a mischievous smile. She looked familiar.

"Penelope, don't dawdle," Aunt Phyllis said, looking in from the hall. "I have a ten o'clock appointment with the dressmaker."

The dressmaker! I thought. *Perhaps Aunt Phyllis will buy me a dress. A red silk dress. With a red silk dress I could audition for a real stage director. I could win a part, even if it was only a small part. Then I could make my stage debut and then the leading lady might get sick and then they would ask me to take her place and then I would become a great star of the theater.*

And when I'd become a great star of the theater, I'd get a suite all to myself at the Palace Hotel, and Aunt Phyllis would have to ask my permission before she could enter the room.

"Penelope!"

"Can we take the cable car to the dressmaker?" I asked, coming into the hall.

"Do you mean *may* we take the cable car?" said Aunt Phyllis, who was standing with Petunia. "No. We will walk. This will be our morning constitutional."

"Please, can't we ride the cable car just this once? It would be such a special treat. Please?"

She didn't say anything. She just looked at me. It was a look that said, "In this household, children do not question the decisions of adults."

"Violet! Aldebaran! We're leaving!" Aunt Phyllis called.

Aldy came flying down the stairs. "I'm here. I'm ready," he said. He huffed and puffed and pulled up his socks. His pudgy cheeks were red.

Aunt Phyllis started to tap her foot. A minute later, Violet started down the stairs. She didn't run. She walked. When she reached the bottom she said, "Sorry, Mother. I was just fixing my petticoats. Do they look all right?"

Aunt Phyllis nodded approvingly.

"All right, everyone, let us go," said Aunt Phyllis, pulling on her hat and gloves.

She picked up her parasol—a fancy, blue affair with little tassels—then handed one to each of us girls. She opened the door. The fog had lifted, and the sun was shining. We started down the street.

"How far is it to the dressmaker?" I asked Aldy.

"A ways."

We reached the corner of Franklin Street and turned left on Sacramento.

"Where is the dressmaker?" I asked Violet.

"Downtown. On Sutter. Where all the fashionable shops are."

I suppose it was obvious from the look on my face that I didn't know where Sutter was. Violet looked shocked.

"You've never been to Sutter Street?" she said. She turned and whispered something to Petunia.

Petunia smirked. "I bet you've never been to comportment class, either," she said.

"I don't need comportment class," I said. "I am an *actress*."

Petunia and Violet burst into laughter. I twirled my parasol and walked a little faster.

We reached Van Ness Avenue, where the houses were even grander than on Aunt Phyllis's street. We turned into a business district. COFFEE AND SPICES, BOOTS AND SHOES, HAY AND GRAIN, the signs said. We passed butchers, grocers, druggists, tailors, bakers, a dentist, a doctor, a lawyer, a banker, a wool merchant. I was beginning to think Aunt Phyllis had picked a hilly route just to make us suffer.

"Are we almost there?" I asked Aldy.

He shrugged.

Just as I thought my legs were going to give out, Aunt Phyllis came to a halt in front of a wooden building. A small sign next to the door said in gold letters: MRS. EUGENIA PLUMBOTTOM, DRESSMAKER.

A little brass bell attached to the doorknob announced our arrival. As we entered, a plump woman with her hair poufed on top of her head came through a door at the back of the shop.

"Mrs. Leuts, I've been expecting you," she said. "I see you've brought the whole family. How lovely." She said it out of the corner of her mouth, as if she didn't think it was lovely at all. "And who is this?"

"This is Penelope Leuts Bailey," said Aunt Phyllis. "My niece. Penelope, this is Mrs. Plumbottom. Penelope is staying with us for several months while her parents are *away*." When she said *away* she drew her lips back in a fake smile.

"How lovely," Mrs. Plumbottom said again. "Well, Mrs. Leuts, let's get on with the fitting. Children, you may sit." She pointed to some tufted chairs. "Keep your hands to yourselves. Mrs. Leuts and I will be in the dressing room."

She walked toward the back of the shop. Aunt Phyllis was about to follow when I touched her on the arm.

"Yes?" she said.

"May I. . . Um, I thought I might need a dress if . . . if . . ."

Aunt Phyllis stared at me, her eyes hard and cold. "If what?" she said.

"If we went to the theater?" I said, in a small voice.

Her eyes flashed. "The theater! Neither I nor any of my children have ever been to the theater. How improper! Violet, keep an eye on your brother and sister." She turned and disappeared into the dressing room.

I sank into a chair and stared at the rug. Out of the corner of my eye I saw Violet pick up an illustrated monthly. Presently, she and Petunia were studying the pictures. I leaned over to see. They were looking at pictures of fashionable ladies promenading through a park.

Aldy sat twiddling his thumbs. Every time he caught me looking at him, he stuck a thumb in the direction of a display of corsets and rolled his eyes. After a while he stood up, walked over to the window, and pointed to some hats that were decorated with ostrich feathers.

"Hey, Penny! Look!" he said.

I joined him, grabbed an enormous hat, and plunked it on his head. Then I lifted a pink feather boa from a hook and threw it around my neck. "How do I look?" I asked, climbing up on a chair. I put a hand on my heart. *"O Romeo, Romeo! wherefore art thou, Romeo?"*

"How do *I* look?" said Aldy, pointing to his head.

"You both look ridiculous!" hissed Violet. "Sit down."

Aldy lifted one end of the boa and waved it at Violet. "Shrinking Violet, shrinking Violet."

Violet rolled her eyes and turned away.

"Moony Petuney, moony Petuney," he said, waving at Petunia.

Petunia jumped up and snatched the end of the boa out of Aldy's hand. The rest of it was still wrapped around my neck. She pulled on it, and for a minute the boa stretched out between Petunia and me like a piece of Turkish taffy, and I started to choke, and then—SNAP!—it broke.

"Look what you did!" screeched Petunia.

"I didn't do anything! You were choking me!" I yelled, jumping off the chair.

"It was your fault, Tuney," said Aldy.

"You started it!" she shouted, giving him a shove.

Mrs. Plumbottom's head poked out of the dressing room door. "What is all this commotion? Can't you children—"

She stopped in mid-sentence. Aldy whipped the hat off his head. Petunia let go of her piece of the boa, and it fluttered to the floor.

"What have you done?" sputtered Mrs. Plumbottom. "You horrid children!"

She stomped to the middle of the room, whisked up the piece of boa, and shook it at us. "You'll pay for this, you little . . . beasts!"

Violet rose from her chair. "Calm down, Mrs. Plumbottom. I'll take care of this."

Mrs. Plumbottom's mouth dropped open.

Violet turned to us. "Does anyone have any money?"

"No," said Aldy.

"No," said Petunia.

"Nor do I," said Violet. "Penny?"

My hand creeped to my pocket. It held the little purse Mama had given me, the one with the dollar bill.

"No," I answered.

Violet narrowed her eyes. "What's that lump in your pocket?"

"Nothing," I said.

Violet grabbed me by the arm, wrested the purse out of my pocket, and tore it open. She held up the dollar bill. "Will this be enough?" she asked Mrs. Plumbottom.

The dressmaker flushed clear to the top of her fancy hairdo. She looked from one to the other of us. Then she snatched the dollar, tucked it into her bosom, and marched back to the dressing room.

I glared at Violet. "My mother gave me that dollar! For an emergency!"

"Aldebaran, don't you dare touch anything else in this shop," said Violet, ignoring me. "You're the one who should be going to comportment class."

"Shut your mouth, Penny, you'll catch a fly," said Petunia. She plumped her petticoats and sat down.

I unwound the remains of the boa and threw it at Violet. It landed on the floor. She picked an invisible speck off her sleeve.

"Never mind her, Penny," said Aldy. "Sit down."

I picked up the boa and hung it on the back of an empty chair. We sat in silence. I was fuming. I'd only been in San Francisco for one day, and already my dollar was gone. I could've wrung Petunia's neck. And Violet's, too.

But the longer I sat, the more I began to worry. If Aunt Phyllis found out about the boa, she'd tell Mama I'd been a bad girl, and I'd never get to have elocution lessons.

"You may deliver the new gowns as soon as they are ready," said Aunt Phyllis, coming out of the dressing room. "Children, come. Good day, Mrs. Plumbottom."

Without looking at us, Aunt Phyllis picked up her parasol and swept out the door. We scrambled after her.

Did she know about the boa?

The walk home felt endless. Aunt Phyllis hurried us along. When we reached the house, she announced that she was going upstairs to change. Halfway up the stairs she came to an abrupt halt.

"Don't think for a minute," she said, "that I don't know what happened at Mrs. Plumbottom's. Violet, you were in charge. Who was responsible for the torn boa?"

"Penny. And Aldy."

"Liar!" said Aldy.

"Aldebaran!" snapped Aunt Phyllis. "Mind your tongue!"

"It was Petunia's fault," he protested.

"That's not true," said Petunia.

"Penelope, what do you have to say for yourself?"

"It wasn't my fault."

"You were the one standing on the chair," said Violet.

"Standing on the chair?" said Aunt Phyllis. "Enough! Penelope and Aldebaran, go to your rooms. Winifred will bring you lunch. Father will deal with you when he gets home. Violet and Petunia, lunch in the dining room in twenty minutes." She marched the rest of the way up the stairs.

Aldy glared at Violet.

"You're in trouble," sneered Petunia. "Ha ha."

He reached out to hit her, but she pulled away. "Stupid," he growled.

"Go away," said Violet, flicking a strand of hair over her shoulder.

Aldy tromped up the stairs, and I followed. When I got to my room, I stood and stared out the window.

Everything is terrible, I thought.

My parents left me. Aunt Phyllis hates me. I'll never be an actress. If this keeps up, I will have to run away.

CHAPTER EIGHT

Punishment

Punishment was scheduled for seven thirty in Uncle Henry's study. Aldy and I filed in at the appointed hour and lined up in front of the fireplace.

Aunt Phyllis sat stiffly on a chair, a sewing basket at her feet. She was working on some needlepoint. She pricked the fabric with sharp jabs of her needle.

Uncle Henry cleared his throat. "We are disappointed, Aldebaran," he began. His deep voice boomed as if from a mountaintop. "This is not the kind of behavior we expected when we invited Penelope to stay with us."

He looked at me for a moment, then turned back to Aldy. "Your mother and I have been discussing an appropriate punishment." He stroked his handlebar mustache. "Less enlightened parents, perhaps, would give you a thrashing. But as you well know, we do not believe in corporal punishment. Your mother feels you should not be allowed to go on the picnic tomorrow."

I winced.

"However." He cleared his throat. "I think something more *definitive* is in order. Something more *character building*, shall we say."

"Your mother and I believe," he went on, "that it is our

God-given duty as parents to mold our children into civilized human beings."

He commenced to stroll back and forth like a Sunday preacher. "We are all born with wild energies," he said, raising an eyebrow in my direction. "However. Hr-hmm. Those of us who by God's grace have been given the opportunity to better ourselves, to make something of our lives, must learn to tame those wild energies. To grasp the bull by the horns. To seize the tiger by the tail, so to speak."

He peered down at Aldy. "Your mother has pointed out that civilizing a child is a difficult business, more easily accomplished with girls." Then he looked at me again. "*Some* girls."

Did he just wink at me?

"Therefore," he went on, "I have decided that you, Aldebaran, having reached the advanced age of eleven, are old enough to accompany me on my annual hunting expedition to the north woods. There, you will learn some discipline. And, God willing, you may obtain some insight into what distinguishes men from beasts."

I couldn't believe it. Aldy had misbehaved, and he was getting to go on an expedition with Uncle Henry! What a stroke of luck!

Or was it? Maybe sharing a tent with Uncle Henry wouldn't be such fun. I glanced at Aldy. I thought I saw a glimmer of a smile on his lips.

I studied Uncle Henry. Then I saw him wink at Aldy. Uncle Henry knew! He knew Aldy would have fun! He knew Aunt Phyllis's rules were—

Aunt Phyllis put down her needlepoint. There was a grave look on her face. Aldy's almost-smile vanished. It wouldn't do for her to think we were taking our punishment lightly. It was clear from the look on her face that she saw no humor in the situation.

She beckoned Uncle Henry with a crook of her finger. He bent down and she whispered something in his ear. He nodded and pulled out his pocket watch. It was attached to a gold chain that draped across his belly. He checked the time, raising one eyebrow as he did so. Then he walked over to his enormous oak desk, pulled some papers out of a drawer, and sat down.

Aunt Phyllis spoke. "That will be all, Aldebaran. Go to your room. Penelope, I will deal with you myself."

As he left, Aldy glanced at me, his face full of pity. Aunt Phyllis rose. I shifted my weight from foot to foot.

"Penelope," she said, "your mother and father have entrusted me with your safety and well-being, a position of trust that I take extremely seriously. Some people,"—she glanced at Uncle Henry—"may find your high spirits attractive, but in the long run that kind of behavior will not serve you well. In this house we expect ladylike behavior from young ladies. *Ladylike* behavior. Not horseplay."

She waited for a moment, looking pleased with her words.

"You are a filly that must be reined in. It is high time that you learned the value of tact and restraint, qualities I find sorely lacking in one as impulsive as yourself. Henceforth, you will conduct yourself in a ladylike manner in public. Is that clear?"

I nodded.

"What did you say?"

"Yes, Aunt Phyllis."

"Furthermore, Penelope, for the remainder of the summer you will be joining Violet and Petunia at their thrice-weekly comportment lessons with Miss Olivia Stipp."

"But I don't need comport—"

"And for goodness sake, child, please refrain from blurting out everything that comes into your mind!"

She sighed, sat, and picked up her needlepoint. "My word, Penelope. You seem to have no comprehension whatsoever of the difficulties that can beset young girls. Standing on a chair and flaunting a feather boa as if you were a—" She shuddered.

"Whatever could you have been thinking?"

I shrugged.

She pulled a thread taut with her needle. "Excuse me?" she said.

"Nothing, Aunt Phyllis. I wasn't thinking anything."

"Precisely. You weren't thinking. From now on we will make certain that your mind is engaged more productively. Here is the Holy Bible. You will stay with us for the rest of the evening and cultivate your mind. You may sit there."

She thrust the Bible at me and pointed to the sofa. I sat down meekly and opened the Bible. My insides were fluttering.

It isn't fair! Aldy doesn't have to go to comportment class. Just because he's a boy.

I felt tears coming on. I pushed them away. I didn't want to cry in front of her.

Why is she so cruel? Am I truly such an awful child?

Mama would never speak to me like that. Mama loves me.

But if she loves me why did she leave me here?

I glanced in Aunt Phyllis's direction. She was picking at a thread. I decided then and there to write another letter to Mama, and this time I would tell her all about Aunt Phyllis. If I told Mama the truth about how Aunt Phyllis was treating me, she'd understand. She'd send money so I could join her and Papa in Hawaii.

Aunt Phyllis looked up, as if she had heard me thinking. "It is quite evident to me," she said, "that your mother and father haven't the slightest—" She interrupted herself and turned to Uncle Henry. "Henry, you simply must speak to your sister when she returns. I can only pray that the damage done to this poor child's character is not permanent."

Uncle Henry raised his hand to acknowledge her words, but didn't look up from his papers.

I frowned and buried my nose in the Bible.

She ought not to criticize Mama. And I don't need comportment class! I already know how to sit like a lady and how to tell which fork is the dessert fork. That torn boa was every bit as much Petunia's fault, and Violet lied about it, and they're not being punished. It's so unfair!

I tried to read, but the longer I sat, the more upset I became.

I'm plenty enough of a lady for Mama and Papa. They don't think I'm a wild horse that needs training, not one whit! They like me the way I am.

I peeked at Aunt Phyllis.

I'll show her. I'll sneak out tomorrow and run away and become an actress.

Well, maybe not tomorrow. Tomorrow is the picnic. Maybe the next day.

The clock ticked. I read. Aunt Phyllis concentrated on her needlepoint. Uncle Henry studied his paperwork. After a while someone knocked on the door, three quick, little raps. The door creaked open, and Winifred came in. She curtsied to Aunt Phyllis and Uncle Henry. Moving silently about the room, she lit the gas lamps one by one. At each set of French doors she untied the gold cord that held back the blue velvet drapes. The heavy drapes fell closed, swaying for a moment like a pendulum and then hanging still. When all the drapes were closed, Winifred curtsied again and left.

I listened to the tick of the clock.

Oh Lord, how long must I sit here? I wish I were reading Romeo and Juliet.

"Try the psalms," said Aunt Phyllis, without looking up.

I leafed through the psalms, looking for one that was short, and my eye settled upon number ninety-three, "The Lord reigneth, he is clothed with majesty." I liked it because it talked about the sea, which made me think of Mama, sailing upon the Pacific. I especially liked the part that said, "The Lord on high is mightier than the noise of many waters, yea, than the mighty waves of the sea." It comforted me to know that God was looking down on Mama and would protect her from the mighty waves. I decided to memorize the psalm so I could add it to my nightly prayers.

By the time the clock struck half past eight, my eyelids were beginning to droop.

When Aunt Phyllis heard the chime she looked up and said, "Penelope, you may be excused." Then she resumed her needlework.

I set the Bible on the sofa.

"Aunt Phyllis?" I said. "I'm going to write a letter to Mama. Do you think we could mail it tomorrow?"

Her needle hung in the air.

"The post office is closed on the Fourth of July," she said. "Tomorrow is the picnic. Be ready to depart at half past nine. And no shenanigans."

CHAPTER NINE

The Beach

The next morning we boarded the Sutro Railroad and rode to the end of the line. The car was crowded with people on holiday, toting blankets and picnic hampers. They jostled each other as they took their seats, but no one complained. Everyone seemed to be in a fine mood, except Aunt Phyllis.

She sat quietly, a disagreeable look on her face. Aldy bounced up and down on the cane seat, and Petunia cuddled up close to Uncle Henry. Violet stared at a handsome young man with slicked-down hair who was trying to jolly some girls across the aisle. Every time he said something, they tittered, hiding their smiles behind gloved hands.

"How do I look?" Violet kept saying, as she fluffed her hair.

"You look fine," I said.

The fourth time she asked, I just rolled my eyes.

We disembarked near a sign that said CLIFF HOUSE—1/4 MILE. Eager for a glimpse of the ocean, I tried to slip ahead of the crowd, but we were caught in the middle of a crush of bodies, and I couldn't break free. I was lugging my parasol and a picnic hamper, too.

"Stay together, children," called Aunt Phyllis.

We reached a corner and waited for some carriages to pass. The wind blew our skirts in all directions. Uncle Henry had to put an arm around skinny Petunia so she wouldn't blow away. Aunt Phyllis looked at me and began clucking about propriety. I

tried to hold my skirts in place for her sake, but to no avail.
Even Aunt Phyllis can't stop the wind.

As we stood there, I heard a great roar and a *whoosh.*

"Aldy! Do you hear it?"

"Hear what?"

"The ocean! Do you hear it?" It was all I could do to keep from running across the street. I thought I would die of impatience. The whole family was moving about as fast as molasses in cold water.

Finally we stepped off the curb. I saw a flash of sun on the water and tore across the road.

"Watch out for the drop!" yelled Uncle Henry.

I pulled up short at the edge of a cliff. Before me lay the Pacific Ocean. The water went on and on, an immense field of gray-green, rolling and dipping and rising like a living, breathing animal. A tiny dot of a clipper ship inched across the horizon. Beneath the cliff, waves crashed onto a sandy beach. Over the whole scene arched an immense blue sky, streaked with white clouds. It was almost perfect. If Mama and Papa had been there, it *would* have been perfect. I took a deep breath of salty air.

Aldy caught up with me. Together we looked at the view.

"Impressive, isn't it?" said Uncle Henry, coming up from behind.

"Let's go down," said Aldy.

"Stay to the path, children," Aunt Phyllis instructed, pointing with her furled parasol. "The cliffs are unstable. Please remember that no one—NO ONE—is allowed near the water. The waves are unpredictable. A child can be snatched away. Like that!" She snapped open her parasol for emphasis. "Let us descend."

We followed a path lined with wild grasses. Aunt Phyllis led the way. When we reached the bottom, she turned to the left and marched about twenty feet across the sand.

"Here," she announced. She unfolded a little stool and sat down. "Children, spread the blankets. Henry, please supervise."

"When do we eat?" asked Aldy.

"Later," said Aunt Phyllis.

We settled into our spot. It was a glorious day. Men, women, and children strolled by in their holiday best. Some sported straw boaters. Red, white, and blue ribbons fluttered off the back of the women's hats. Many of the men had tiny American flags in their hat bands. Down the beach some boys were playing hoops. Small children dug in the sand.

"Altogether a delightful atmosphere, don't you think, my dear?" said Uncle Henry.

"Very festive," Aunt Phyllis said with a sniff.

Aldy whispered in my ear, "Mother doesn't like the beach."

I looked at him and my mouth dropped open. "No!"

"Yes!" He turned to Uncle Henry. "Father, may Penny and I take a walk?"

Uncle Henry raised his index finger and pointed to the sky. "As long as you do not go near the water."

"Huzzah!" said Aldy. "C'mon, Penny!"

He grabbed my arm and we set off down the beach.

"Penelope! Your parasol!" called Aunt Phyllis, but I pretended not to hear.

After a few minutes I turned to Aldy. "Why not?" I said.

"Why not what?"

"Why doesn't your mother like the beach?"

"I don't know."

"But *how* could she not like the beach?"

"I don't know. She says the sand gets in her shoes and the sun spoils her face."

I vowed to myself that I would never, ever be like Aunt Phyllis.

We walked for a while in silence. I began to wonder if there was any way I could get out of going to comportment class. I pictured myself in white gloves, perched at the edge of a hard sofa, my knees clamped together, my feet at an angle, just so. I imagined an endless lecture about who gets introduced to whom, and how, and when, and why. The indignity of it! Me, the budding actress, forced to take etiquette lessons!

"I'm starving," said Aldy.

"You're always starving," I pointed out. "Tag, you're it!" I yelled, and raced down the beach. I let him catch up with me, then I jumped on him, leaping into the air and knocking him down. We fell in a heap, laughing.

"I'm hungry," he said, when we had finished laughing. "Isn't it lunchtime yet?"

"No," I said, stretching out on the sand.

He stood and dribbled sand on me. The grains bounced off my arm.

I got up. "Let's walk a little farther," I said.

We walked for a while. I collected some shells. We were about to turn back when I spotted a group of boys and girls tumbling down a path onto the beach.

"Look," I said. "What a strange girl."

At the front of the group was a girl about Violet's age. She wore an odd outfit that seemed as if it were made of silk scarves, sewn together at strange angles. The fabric fluttered about her knees when she walked. But she didn't truly walk—she flowed across the sand, waving her arms in grand, sweeping motions like an actress declaiming a speech. She called to the children behind her, but I couldn't make out her words because of the roar of the surf.

The children spilled onto the beach, higgledy-piggledy. There must have been ten or twelve of them. They laughed and shouted like a jolly band of ragamuffins. Each had a scarf around his neck and another at his waist. Scarves were tucked into hats and came spilling out of pockets. Not one of the girls had a parasol.

When they were all assembled on the beach they began to remove their shoes.

"Oh, Aldy, they're taking off their shoes! Let's!"

In a flash our shoes were off. We approached the group.

The girl had mounted a rock.

"We assemble as a mighty band of spirits," she said. "For

today, on the Fourth of July, we celebrate a birth—the birth of our nation! And so we have come down to the sea, from whence all life emerged, to pay obeisance to the spirits of the deep. The power of the sea is our power. See the motion of her waves! Feel the pull of her tides!"

She raised her hands above her head and waved them slowly from side to side. All the children did the same.

"May the heartbeat of Mother Ocean stir the blood that runs in your veins. With our sinews shall we carry out her commands! As the seaweed clings to the rock, we cling to thee, oh mighty Mother Ocean!"

She unwrapped a scarf from round her neck, held it high in the air, and leapt off the rock. "Bow down to the Mother of all Mothers!" she cried, bowing so deeply toward the ocean that her face almost touched the sand. The children bowed, too. Then, without looking up, she twisted her hand with a little flourish, and her scarf rippled like a snake.

She straightened, and with a great cry ran toward the water, yelling, "To the ocean, ye spirits of the deep!"

At her cry the children ran toward the water, screaming and laughing and pushing and waving scarves in the air. Aldy and I watched, dumbstruck. I had never heard nor seen anything quite like this strange girl and her band of followers, and I wagered Aldy hadn't either. *Were they actually going to enter the water?*

Just then a large wave broke, and a small boy with chestnut curls was knocked off his feet. The girl snatched him from the ocean's jaws and came running up the beach toward where we stood. She placed the crying child on the sand and began rummaging through a pile of bags and garments that the children had dropped. The bottom of her scarf-dress was dripping wet. With her windblown hair, she looked like a sea nymph.

We edged closer.

"Have you a blanket?" she asked, looking up. I caught a glimpse of her eyes—green and brown and gold and mysterious.

47

"Um, uh,—" said Aldy.

"No," I said. "We left everything back at—"

"Never mind. It's all right." She sank onto the sand and wrapped herself around the little boy.

The other children came straggling back from the water's edge and huddled around. The little boy who had fallen into the water snuggled into her arms. She wiggled her nose into his neck and he giggled and squealed.

"He's fine," she assured the other children, and sang them a little song. Then she turned to me. "What's your name?"

"Penelope. And this is Aldebaran."

She put the little boy down, got to her feet, and bowed. "Welcome to the Fourth of July."

I bowed back. Aldy just stood there. I tugged on his arm, and he bowed.

"*Princess* Penelope, that is," I said. "And *Prince* Aldebaran. At your service." I reached into my pocket and pulled out my shells. "Our gift to you, Empress," I said, dropping the shells at her feet.

She took a deep breath, raised her arms straight out in front of her, and held them there as if they were floating. Then she opened her arms and bowed again. "I'm Isabelle," she said. "Isabelle Grey."

I grinned. Here was someone who would be at home on the stage, just like me.

"We ought to go," said Aldy. "Lunch."

"Do you come here often?" I said to Isabelle.

"All the time. These are my dancing students."

"C'mon, Penny," said Aldy. "Mother's waiting."

"I know, I know." I turned to Isabelle. "Perhaps we will meet again."

As Aldy and I walked away, I turned and bowed again. "Fare thee well, noble Empress! Good-bye, ye worshippers of the sea!"

The children lifted their scarves and waved. "Good-bye, Princess Penelope! Good-bye, Prince Aldebaran! Good-bye!"

CHAPTER TEN

Miss Stipp

"I bet she's an actress," I said to Aldy when we got home. "Where do you think she lives? Do you think we'll ever see her again? Aldy, I am starved for the theater. Starved! Are you sure you don't want to make up a play with me?"

"Nah," he said.

I began to hatch a secret plan. If there were actors living next door, I was going to meet them, even if I had to meet them in my nightdress.

Early the next morning I tiptoed down the back stairs and out the kitchen door. The sky was streaked with the pink of dawn, and the ground was cold beneath my bare feet. I peered over the hedge into the neighbors' garden. It was filled with blooming rose bushes, their colors dim in the morning light. On the patio, a wrought iron table and chairs were covered with dew.

I slipped through the hedge and crept up to the house. There was no one in sight. I peeked through a window. All was quiet inside. I slipped a note under the door.

Dear Mr. and Mrs. Prenderwinkel,

I am staying next door with my aunt and uncle while my parents are away. My cousin Aldy told me you are actors. I would like to meet you because I want to be an actor, too. Please let me know when you will be at home but do not tell Aunt Phyllis. I will look for you in the garden.

Sincerely,

Penelope Leuts Bailey

I flew back to my room. Now that I had introduced myself, surely I was on my way to becoming an actress. I twirled in front of the mirror.

> *O Romeo, Romeo! wherefore are thou, Romeo?*
> *Deny thy father and refuse thy —*

A rap on the door interrupted my speech. It was Aunt Phyllis, reminding me in no uncertain terms that this was the morning I was condemned to start comportment class with Miss Olivia Stipp.

I barely had time for breakfast before Aunt Phyllis hurried us out the door.

"Is it far?" I asked Aunt Phyllis.

"A brisk walk," she said.

By the time we finished what Aunt Phyllis called a brisk walk, my hands were cold and damp with nervousness. We approached the gray, stone building, and entered a large foyer that smelled of furniture wax and perfume. Mothers and daughters stood in little groups, waiting for the class to begin. Violet and Petunia rushed to greet some other girls. I stood close to Aunt Phyllis and tried to look as if I belonged.

"Good day, Eugenia," said Aunt Phyllis, greeting a friend.

"Good morning, Phyllis."

"Lovely day, Lydia, is it not?" said Aunt Phyllis to another. "And how are you, Millicent?"

"Fine, thank you, and you?"

"We are well, thank you," said Aunt Phyllis. "Allow me to introduce my niece, Penelope Leuts Bailey. Penelope, this is Mrs. Browner, Mrs. Dunst, and Mrs. Low."

"How do you do?" I said, hoping I didn't sound as awkward as I felt.

The ladies looked me up and down. I felt small.

A door slid open, and we were shown into a ballroom. Big brass chandeliers hung from the ceiling, and dark wooden chairs with brown leather seats were lined up against the walls. A grand piano stood in one corner. Aunt Phyllis marched me up to a short, round, gray-haired lady who was standing near the door. Her dress was the color of a rusty nail.

"Miss Stipp, I've a new charge for you this morning," said Aunt Phyllis. "May I present my niece, Miss Penelope Leuts Bailey. Penelope, this is Miss Stipp."

Miss Stipp lowered her chin and raised what I guessed was a lorgnette to her face. I knew about lorgnettes from novels, but I had never seen one in person. The thick glass lenses made her eyes look enormous.

"How do you do?" she said.

She lowered the lorgnette and offered me a gloved hand. I shook it. Her handshake was very firm.

"Behave," said Aunt Phyllis. "I will return at noon." She followed the other mothers out the door.

Miss Stipp clapped her hands. The room fell silent.

"Attention, please! Take your seats. No rushing. A lady sits in a leisurely manner. Spine erect, knees together, hands on lap."

Everyone sat. I glanced around. There were some twenty or thirty girls. Violet was one of the oldest, and Petunia one of the youngest.

"You may remove your gloves."

Each girl took off her gloves, placed them on her lap, and

held out her hands, palms down. I did the same, though I didn't know why. Miss Stipp stood at the end of the row of chairs on the other side of the room. She took a deep breath, raised her lorgnette, and sailed down the row, inspecting each girl's nails.

I heard a whisper. It was coming from the girl next to me.

"Are you new?"

Without taking my eyes off Miss Stipp, I nodded.

"I'm Consuela," said the voice.

I looked at her and was met with a steady gaze. Her eyes were big and brown, her face framed with thick, black hair.

"Consuela Hopkins." She smiled.

I smiled back. "Hi," I whispered. "I'm Penny Bailey."

Miss Stipp glanced in our direction, then went back to examining nails.

"You get used to it," whispered Consuela.

"Used to what?"

"The General."

"General who?"

"General Stipp." She nodded her head in Miss Stipp's direction.

I giggled.

Miss Stipp crossed the room and started down our row. As she approached, my stomach started to flutter. Three girls down from me, she stopped.

"Theodosia," she said. "Your nails are too long."

The girl named Theodosia blushed.

"Come with me, please."

Miss Stipp led Theodosia to a corner of the room and pulled a small pair of scissors out of her pocket. Everybody watched as she clipped Theodosia's nails and let them fall into a basket. I looked at my nails and hoped Miss Stipp would approve. I would rather die than be made a laughingstock in front of all these girls.

Theodosia sat down, and Miss Stipp resumed her inspection. She seemed to hesitate for a moment as she passed in front of me, but she didn't stop.

When she was through with her inspection she walked over to the piano. A thin, old lady in a plain, gray dress was perched on the edge of the piano bench. She looked like a small, frail mouse. As Miss Stipp came closer, the lady began to blink rapidly. Miss Stipp put down her lorgnette and picked up a wooden stick that lay upon the piano lid. With the point of the stick she lifted the long drapery that covered the piano.

"Girls, what do you see under the piano?"

There was silence in the room. She banged her stick on the floor.

"Who can tell me, please?"

Consuela and I looked at each other. A girl at the end of the row raised her hand.

"Yes, Melba?" said Miss Stipp.

Melba stood. "Piano legs?" she said.

Someone giggled.

"Silence!" thundered Miss Stipp. "You are mistaken, Melba. These are piano *limbs*. It is just as improper to refer to 'the legs' of a piano as it is to refer to 'the legs' of a woman. In both cases it is preferable to say 'limbs.' 'Limbs' is a much more cultivated turn of phrase, suited to the tender sensibilities of the weaker sex."

Consuela rolled her eyes at me. I smiled back.

Miss Stipp spoke again. "Thank you, Melba, you may sit down. Girls, take your books and line up!"

The girls rose and went over to a table upon which books were piled. I took a book and stood in line next to Consuela.

Miss Stipp clapped her hands twice. "Music, please!" she said to the woman at the piano.

The old lady attacked the keys, swaying to and fro in an exaggerated manner.

"Who is that strange lady at the piano?" I asked Consuela.

"That's *Mrs.* Stipp, the General's mother," she answered.

I started to giggle. "Do you mean she's Mrs. General?"

Consuela giggled, too.

"A stately processional, please," said Miss Stipp, clapping again. "Girls, you may proceed."

Mrs. Stipp struck up a serious tune and we began to walk across the room, balancing our books on our heads. On every beat Miss Stipp banged her stick against the floor.

"On the *beat*, girls! Pay *attention* to the *rhythm*! Ears alive!"

I was very good at balancing a book on my head, on account of Mama's exercises. Miss Stipp nodded approvingly. By the time we had walked back and forth a few times, I was feeling very pleased with myself.

Miss Stipp struck the floor with her stick, and the music stopped. "Miss Leuts. Penelope, is it? Step forward, please. Girls, a demonstration. Our new student is putting you all to shame. Please notice Penelope's posture."

I could feel my face grow warm. I stole a look at Consuela. She smiled in sympathy.

Miss Stipp nodded, and the music began again. She motioned with her stick for me to walk down the line of girls. Suddenly my knees were a-wobble and my shoulders began to shake.

Out of the corner of my eye I could see Petunia whispering to Violet.

"On the *beat*, Penelope!" barked Miss Stipp.

I concentrated on my feet. As I approached Violet, the book teetered atop my head. Miss Stipp pounded the rhythm with her stick. I kept walking. I passed Petunia, and she coughed. My step faltered. I put out my arms to steady myself, and the book tilted and fell, hitting the floor with a loud thump. Petunia smiled.

"Thank you, Penelope, that will be all," said Miss Stipp,

frowning. "You may rejoin the line."

My cheeks were burning as I took my place. I wondered what other tortures Miss Stipp was planning.

She answered that question straightaway by launching into a speech about the benefits of good posture. We stood in line for what felt like an hour. By the time she was finished, I vowed I would never stand up straight again, ever.

I could hear voices in the hall outside. The elderly Mrs. Stipp struck some chords on the piano.

"Twelve o'clock, girls!" said Miss Stipp. She opened the ballroom doors and we poured into the foyer.

I said good-bye to Consuela. She stood arm-in-arm with her mother, a beautiful woman with jet black hair.

"Do you come every week?" I asked Consuela.

"Yes," she said. "Three times."

"Me, too," I said. I lowered my voice. "I don't know how I'll bear it."

She looked surprised. I wondered if she would still be my friend if she knew I wanted to be an actress.

"Let's be friends," said Consuela, smiling.

"Okay," I said, smiling back.

"Penelope?" Aunt Phyllis's voice cut through the din. She was standing in the corner, talking to Miss Stipp.

I made my way toward her.

". . . posture isn't bad but she talks out of turn," Miss Stipp was saying.

"Hrmph," said Aunt Phyllis. "Penelope, come. Violet, Petunia."

We followed Aunt Phyllis into the street.

Petunia turned to me. "I see you made a new friend," she said.

"Oh?" said Aunt Phyllis. "And who would that be?"

"Penelope made friends with Consuela Santiago Hop-skins, Mother," said Petunia, wrinkling her nose.

"Hopkins, Tuney," said Violet. "Not Hop-skins."

"That half-caste Roman Catholic girl?" sniffed Aunt Phyllis. "I see your taste in people is as questionable as your—"

Before she could finish her sentence, a carriage careened around the corner and we had to jump out of the way to avoid being squashed.

"Watch where you are going, sir!" Aunt Phyllis shouted at the driver, as she shook her parasol at him. "Girls, are you all right? Penelope, straighten your skirt. Petunia, you dropped your handkerchief. Violet, your hair."

Violet's hand flew to her head. "What's the matter with my hair?"

"Nothing, darling, nothing, a little mussed, that's all," said Aunt Phyllis. "Come along now." She snapped open her parasol and led the way down the street.

The day had turned cooler. I put my hands in my pockets. My letters!

"Aunt Phyllis, may we stop at the post office, please?"

"It is a trifle out of our way, Penelope."

"Yes, but—"

"I will thank you not to say 'yes, but' to me," she said. "It is a phrase I particularly dislike."

"Yes, but—"

"PENELOPE!"

"Sorry," I mumbled.

"I suppose on this one occasion it would be all right to take a detour. We could use the extra fresh air. To the post office, then."

Violet and Petunia groaned.

"Oh, thank you, Aunt Phyllis!" I said.

"Oh, thank you, Aunt Phyllis!" said Petunia under her breath. Violet laughed.

We walked for a while, then entered a wooden building. As I

handed the letters to the postmaster, I felt a pang of sadness. It would be weeks before I received any letters in return. Mama's boat would arrive in the islands in August. Even if she mailed a letter the day she arrived, it would likely be September by the time it reached San Francisco.

After the post office we went straight home. I tried to corner Winifred before lunch to find out if any message had come from the Prenderwinkels, but I couldn't get her alone. It wasn't until lunch was over that I was able to excuse myself and slip into the kitchen. Mrs. Campbell and Winifred were doing the dishes.

"Did anyone call for me?" I asked.

"No, missy," said Mrs. Campbell.

"No messages? Nothing?"

They both shook their heads.

Disappointed, I wandered back to the parlor. Aldy asked if I wanted to play pirates, but Aunt Phyllis crushed that idea right away.

"It is time to practice for our musicale on Sunday," she announced.

"What musical?" I said.

Violet rolled her eyes. "Not MU-sical. Musi-CAL."

"Practice what?" I said.

Aunt Phyllis looked surprised. "Your instrument, of course."

"But I don't play anything."

"You do not play any musical instruments? *None?*"

"I can sing. And dance the cancan. See—" I lifted my skirts and was about to start kicking my legs when she interrupted.

"Penelope! Stop it this minute! The cancan! Where on earth did you learn such behavior? Has Berkeley, California, become a den of iniquity?"

Violet snorted. Petunia smirked.

"Girls!" said Aunt Phyllis.

"A den of what?" I said.

"Never mind. I'll thank you not to mention the cancan in my house. We will hear your singing later."

I followed Aldy up the stairs.

"What's a musicale?" I said.

"We do it two or three times a year. Everybody comes over, and we perform for them."

"Everybody who?"

"Mother and Father's friends."

I went to my room, picked up Miranda, and dusted her off. I thought about all the songs I knew and how much I loved to sing, especially with Mama. Mama and I could even sing in harmony. I thought of our laughing together as we sang, "Who Threw the Overalls in Mrs. Murphy's Chowder?" Maybe I could sing that at the musicale.

Thinking of Mama, my throat started to tighten. I struggled to fight back tears. But why should I feel sorry for myself? We were having a musicale. Aunt Phyllis might disapprove of acting, but she was going to let me sing, and in front of an audience. It was almost as good as acting. For now.

CHAPTER ELEVEN

"Oh Lonesome Soul"

First thing the next morning I flew down to the kitchen to ask Mrs. Campbell if there were any messages from the Prenderwinkels.

"Not a word, Missy," she said.

I dragged myself back to my room.

"Miranda," I said, picking up my doll, "I can't stand it. There are actors living right next door, and I can't manage to meet them."

Frustrated, I marched down to the backyard with my Shakespeare book and took up a lookout post on the pirate ship. I tried to read, but every few minutes I kept jumping up and peering over the hedge, hoping to see the neighbors. I didn't see so much as a chipmunk.

It was discouraging, but I didn't give up hope. Perhaps the Prenderwinkels were away on tour.

After a while I wandered inside. There were noises in the parlor. I tiptoed to the door and peeked in. Petunia was standing in front of a music stand, a violin tucked under her chin. Violet sat at the piano bench like a queen on a throne.

"Begin again at D," Violet commanded, pointing to the music.

Petunia lifted her violin bow, and Violet began to play.

"Wait!" cried Petunia. "I wasn't ready!"

Violet stopped. "You're supposed to watch, and take your cue from me," she said. She cracked her knuckles and fluffed her curls. Petunia made a face and lifted her bow again. This time she kept an eye on Violet, and when Violet nodded, they both began to play. Violet's touch was heavy on the keys, and she couldn't keep a steady rhythm, but a lovely sound was flowing from Petunia's violin. I listened in surprise.

Petunia stopped. "You played a wrong note." She pointed to the music with her bow. "Right there."

Violet sighed. "It's not like *you* play right notes all the time, Miss Perfect."

They began again. This time they got all the way through the piece. The tune set my toes tapping. They played it again. I put down my Shakespeare and started to twirl around the hallway. It felt so good to dance. I made up a little rhyme and sang along.

Two little sisters playing on the ground,
Da-ditty-dum-dum-da-da-da,
One fell up and one fell down,
Traaaaa-la-la-la-la-la.
One little sister sitting on my knee,
Da-ditty-dum-dum-da-da-da,
Pretty as a bird in a banyan tree,
Traaaaa-la-la-la-la-la.

I lifted my skirts and skipped from one end of the hall to the other. I came back the other way with a shuffle and a hop. I added some fancy things for my elbows, and before long I had a whole dance. I was so busy with my steps I didn't notice that the music in the parlor had stopped. Suddenly I heard a roar of laughter.

"Violet, come see! Penny fancies herself a dancer!"

I froze. Petunia stumbled through the door, looked at me,

and doubled up with laughter.

"What are you talking about, you silly goose?" Violet said from inside the parlor.

"Violet, Penny made up the most foolish little dance. It was so . . . *quaint*! I'd like to see her perform that at the Dunsworth's party next week!" She laughed again.

I felt like shrinking into a little ball.

Violet appeared. "Stop fussing, Tuney," she said. "Who says you're going to that party? You're not even old enough. C'mon. We have more practicing to do."

"But you should have seen Penny prancing about."

Violet grabbed Petunia's wrist.

"Ow! You're hurting me!" Petunia yelled, as Violet dragged her back to the parlor.

I snatched my Shakespeare and ran for the stairs. Taking them two at a time, I fled to my room and slammed the door.

Those two monsters! They ruin everything!

A knock on the door made me jump.

Aldy poked his head into the room. "Want to play?"

"No," I said. "Yes. I don't know."

"Pirates?" he said.

"Not unless your sisters can be the victims."

He laughed. "They won't play with us. They never play pirates. That's why I play with you."

"I don't want to play with them, anyway. I'd rather play Shakespeare."

"Shakespeare?"

"You're Romeo and I'm Juliet," I said, tossing him my Shakespeare book. "Act II, Scene II."

"But—"

"*Complete Works of Shakespeare.*" Page one thousand seventy four." I climbed onto a chair. "I'm at the window, you're down below in the garden." I struck a pose.

"Oh, all right," he said. He opened the book and found his place. *"But, soft! what light through yonder window breaks?"* he read, in a dull voice. *"It is the east, and Juliet is the sun!—Arise, fair sun, and kill the envious moon—"*

He interrupted himself. "Can I skip some? This is a long speech."

"All right, all right," I said. "I'll come in with my lines." I resumed my pose.

> *O Romeo, Romeo! wherefore art thou, Romeo?*
> *Deny thy father and refuse thy name;*
> *Or, if thou wilt not, be but sworn my love,*
> *And I'll no longer be a Capulet.*

"Now you're supposed to come closer," I whispered.

He took a step nearer. *"Shall I hear more, or shall I speak at this?"* he said.

"'Tis but thy name that is my enemy;" I said.

> *O, be some other name!*
> *What's in a name? that which we call a rose,*
> *By any other name would smell as sweet.*

"You skipped a part," said Aldy.

"Never mind," I said. "Go on."

"I take thee at thy word;" he said. *"Call me but love, and—"*

He interrupted himself again. "Didn't Shakespeare write some plays with pirates?"

"Oh, come on, Aldy."

"Or robbers?" He threw up an arm. "Halt, ye brigands and thieves!"

"What's wrong with *Romeo and Juliet?*"

"It's for girls!" he said. "I'm going outside."

"Wait!" I yelled. I ran after him and almost crashed into Aunt Phyllis.

"Why were you yelling?" she said.

"I didn't mean to," I answered. "We were just practicing."

"Good. I'm glad to see you're taking our little musicale seriously. Perhaps you've been inspired by Petunia. She is so talented."

"Not music. Shakespeare."

I smiled. Adults usually like it when I mention Shakespeare.

Aunt Phyllis frowned. "Why?" she said.

"Why what?" I said.

"*Why* were you practicing Shakespeare?" She tilted her head, waiting for me to answer. Her face made my stomach flutter.

"Because . . . uh . . ."

"Your mother told me about your ridiculous notion to become an actress. Let me tell you something, Penelope Leuts Bailey—"

"It's not ridiculous!"

"I will not have any niece of mine on the stage!"

We glared at each other.

She grasped my arm. "It's time to practice your song," she said. She marched me downstairs to the parlor.

"What I had in mind," she said, "was something on the order of 'Drink to Me Only With Thine Eyes.'"

I groaned. She raised an eyebrow.

"Perhaps you would prefer 'We Strolled the Pebbly Path Where the Bleeding Heart Doth Lie?'"

"Can't I sing something a little faster?" I said. "Do you know the piano part for 'Who Threw the Overalls in Mrs.—'"

"I should have known," she said, shaking her head. "Whoever put that ridiculous song into your head?"

I said nothing. She didn't deserve an answer.

She ignored my silence and leafed through some sheet music.

Finally she pulled out a song. "Here we are," she said. "This will do."

At the top of the sheet was written "Oh Lonesome Soul, Where Hast Thou Flown?"

Aunt Phyllis played a few chords, then nodded for me to begin. I kept my mouth shut.

"Here is where you come in, Penelope," she said, pointing to the music.

"I don't know this song," I said.

"Very well, I will sing it for you first."

She began to sing in a low, wobbly voice that rattled the windows. When the song was over, she waited, as if expecting a compliment. I said nothing. She frowned and started playing the piano part again from the beginning. When she reached the spot where I was supposed to sing, she nodded for me to come in.

I began to sing.

> *Oh lonesome soul, where hast thou flown?*
> *Beyond the shores of distant lands,*
> *'Neath cloudy skies the weeds have grown,*
> *Beyond the reach of loving hands.*

"Yes," said Aunt Phyllis, adding a flourish to the piano part. To my surprise, her playing was quite accomplished. "Now the chorus, then the second verse."

I continued on, through the second, third, fourth, and fifth verses. Aunt Phyllis kept nodding her head and adding little grace notes and trills to the piano part. By the end she was almost smiling. When the piano notes faded, there was an awkward silence. I thought she had liked my singing, but all she did was clear her throat and say, "That will do."

"Aunt Phyllis?" I said. "Must I sing every single verse? I wouldn't want to bore your guests. That part about the meadow—"

"My guests are never bored," she said. "Let me see you

curtsy, please. When you finish the song, you must curtsy."

I crossed one foot behind the other and bobbed my knees.

"That will do," she said again. "We will practice once more just before the guests arrive tomorrow."

I stood there in silence while she shuffled through the sheets of music.

What a stupid song.

At least I'll be performing. I suppose it's good practice for the theater.

I began to wonder what I should wear for this musicale. Certainly Violet would put on a new dress after church. She was constantly changing her clothes.

I counted my outfits in my head. It didn't take long. I didn't have that many, what with the price of fabric and the hours it took Mama to sew everything. Three white blouses and two skirts, one calico and one gray. A few pinafores. A navy dress for everyday, a yellow one for dinner at home, the green striped one for visiting. Mama said to save my brown dress for church. She never mentioned any musicale.

Aunt Phyllis busied herself rearranging the music. I think she forgot I was there.

"You may go," she said, dismissing me with a wave of her hand.

I started toward the door and had my hand on the doorknob when she spoke again.

"If you haven't anything suitable to wear, you may borrow a dress from one of your cousins."

"Thank you, Aunt Phyllis," I said.

Borrow from Violet and Petunia? I thought. *I'd rather wear nothing!*

CHAPTER TWELVE

The Musicale

After church on Sunday we dined quickly, for preparations had to be made for the musicale. Aunt Phyllis was in a snit because she thought Mrs. Stanford had snubbed her at church. Mrs. Stanford, it seemed, was a society lady whom Aunt Phyllis was always trying to impress. Fortunately, Uncle Henry had smoothed Aunt Phyllis's ruffled feathers by the time the guests began to arrive at a quarter past three. Winifred greeted them at the door, curtsying each time she took a lady's shawl or a gentleman's hat and cane. I was introduced to so many people I couldn't remember their names. Soon the parlor was buzzing. I began to feel a buzz in my stomach, too.

What if they don't like my singing?

Will they laugh?

How will I ever be an actress if performing makes me nervous?

Aunt Phyllis instructed me to sit in the front row between Aldy and Petunia. When the grandfather clock struck half past three, she clapped her hands. The room fell silent.

"Good afternoon," she said, with a quick, little smile. "It is with great pleasure that Mr. Leuts and I welcome you to our Summer Musicale." She glanced at Uncle Henry, who was standing near the fireplace. He beamed.

"This afternoon we present a special treat," she continued.

"Our three darlings will be joined by their cousin, Penelope." She nodded in my direction and everyone turned to look at me. I could feel my cheeks flush.

"Dear Penelope is staying with us for several months while her parents are away on a *scientific* expedition." She looked around the room. Perhaps she expected people to be impressed, but no one said anything. Then she continued. "Penelope has been left in our care. I suppose one might say that our dear niece is a *temporary orphan.*" She waited again, thinking she had made a joke. A few people laughed politely. I wanted to melt right down into my shoes and disappear.

"And now, dear friends, without further ado, let us begin. Violet? Petunia?"

Violet and Petunia rose from their seats. Petunia gripped her violin by the neck and walked stiffly to the piano. Violet didn't look nervous at all, not a whit. She settled herself on the bench and adjusted her skirt with much fanfare. Then she struck a note so that Petunia could tune her violin. As Petunia tuned, people chatted quietly, their heads bent together in twos and threes. With so many people in the room, it was a trifle warm. Ladies began to wave handkerchiefs in front of their faces. I watched a little boy in knickers swing his feet back and forth, back and forth, under his chair.

Finally Violet and Petunia were ready. Violet announced the piece—a Mozart sonata. Then she held her hands over the piano keys, and Petunia raised her bow. With a nod from Violet, they began.

As soon as Petunia dug into the strings, her nervousness disappeared. The piece was quite melodious, and as she swayed with the music, people began to smile. At one point Violet hit a wrong note, but Petunia kept playing. The notes of the violin danced about the room.

Even Aunt Phyllis was smiling. She looked happy, almost

relaxed. Suddenly I realized that the pretty, young woman whose portrait hung in the dining room was Aunt Phyllis. It amazed me to think she had once been young. Perhaps she hadn't always been such a sourpuss.

When the piece was over, people clapped warmly. Violet and Petunia curtsied, then sat down in their seats in the front row. I turned to Aldy.

"How did Petunia get to be so good?" I asked.

He shrugged. "Born that way, I guess. Mother's very proud. It drives Violet crazy with jealousy. She practices and practices but she'll never be as good. And Petunia never lets her forget it."

I wondered how someone who made such lovely music could have such an unpleasant personality.

"Are you nervous?" I said. "Who's next, do you think?"

"Me," he said. "Then you."

I squeezed his hand.

"Break a leg," I said.

"What?"

"That's what actors say to each other before they go on the stage."

"I'm not an actor."

"It still counts," I said.

"And now," said Aunt Phyllis, "Aldebaran will play a selection by Stephen Foster, arranged for the clarinet."

Aldy rose from his chair. His cheeks colored up. He fumbled with the parts of his clarinet as he tried to fit them together. I crossed my fingers, hoping he would play well. When he finally started in on his piece, it wasn't bad at all. I clapped long and hard.

"Phew," he said, as he sat down.

My palms were damp. "Do you think people will laugh at me?" I said. "I wish your mother wasn't making me sing 'Oh Lonesome Soul.' I wish I could've sung 'Who Put the Overalls in Mrs. Murphy's Chowder.'"

"That would've been more fun," he agreed.

Petunia poked me. "You're next, Miss Penelope," she said in a mocking tone. "Let's see how good you sing."

"How well she sings," corrected Violet.

"Good. Well. Who cares?" said Petunia. "She can't play the violin like me."

Aunt Phyllis sat at the piano and announced my song. I felt butterflies in my stomach.

Courage, Penelope. The great actress Sarah Bernhardt does this every night.

I swallowed. I cleared my throat. I faced my audience. Thirty expectant faces gazed back at me, all except for one elderly gentleman in the corner. He had fallen asleep.

Aunt Phyllis launched into the introductory chords.

Oh lonesome soul, where hast thou flown?
Beyond the shores of distant lands,
'Neath cloudy skies the weeds have grown,
Beyond the reach of loving hands.

At first my voice shook a little, but by the chorus I could feel myself gaining confidence. I didn't look at the audience but stared at a spot on the wall behind them. I imagined myself on the stage of a huge theater. The music filled my heart, and my voice soared. By the time the song was over, I felt positively covered in glory.

The applause was enthusiastic. Even Aunt Phyllis smiled. I didn't curtsy but took a grand bow, then another, and another. The longer they clapped, the better I felt. Then Aunt Phyllis looked at me as if to say, "That's enough, Penelope," so I took my seat and heaved a sigh of relief.

"Quite the performer, aren't you?" said Violet.

Petunia made a face. "It wasn't so good. I don't know why they clapped so long."

"You wouldn't understand, Petuney," said Aldy. "Because she's so much better than you."

"No one's better than me," said Petunia. "Go walk a gang-plank."

"It's unbecoming to be boastful," said Violet.

"You only say that because you're jealous," said Petunia.

"Oh?" said Violet, pinching her on the arm.

"Ow!" said Petunia.

I smiled at Aldy. "Thanks for sticking up for me."

"Ladies and gentlemen, I have an announcement," said Aunt Phyllis. "Petunia has been accepted into the children's program at the music conservatory. Our little prodigy will begin studies with Professor Entwhistle in the fall."

The audience applauded. Petunia smiled. She rose from her seat and nodded to the audience, then sat back down and poked Violet with her elbow. Violet looked at her with a face that could have curdled milk. Petunia turned to Aldy and stuck out her tongue. "And now, please join us for refreshments," said Aunt Phyllis.

"Are we done?" I asked Aldy.

"With the music. Now we're supposed to circulate."

"What do you mean?"

"Move around."

Everyone rose and headed for the dining room. Aldy helped himself to a handful of cookies. I began to circulate.

"Your singing was lovely, dear," said an elderly woman who looked like she was dressed in her drawing room drapes.

"Thank you," I said.

"Like a songbird," she said, smiling.

I felt myself blush.

Aunt Phyllis rushed over. "My dear Mrs. Crocker," she said.

"Mrs. Leuts," said the woman.

"Did you enjoy Petunia's playing?" asked Aunt Phyllis.

"Your niece is quite talented, too," said Mrs. Crocker.

"We are so proud of our Petunia," gushed Aunt Phyllis. "What an honor to be accepted at the conservatory."

"She should join the choir when she's older," said Mrs. Crocker.

"You're quite right," said Aunt Phyllis. "She can not only play the violin, she has a lovely voice, too."

"I meant your niece," said Mrs. Crocker.

"Oh. Well. Of course," sputtered Aunt Phyllis.

"And where are your brothers and sisters while your parents are away?" asked Mrs. Crocker, turning to me.

"I don't have any."

"What a shame."

"It's not so bad. Sometimes my father takes me to the theater—"

"Do not contradict your elders, Penelope," interrupted Aunt Phyllis. "Please excuse my niece, Mrs. Crocker. Her manners do leave something to be desired." She took Mrs. Crocker by the arm and began to lead her away. "I do hope you'll come back for our Fall Musicale. I'm sure Petunia's playing will be even more outstanding once she starts lessons with Professor Entwhistle at the conservatory."

"Professor Entwhistle? Indeed!" said Mrs. Crocker.

"Go play with your cousins," said Aunt Phyllis, glaring at me over her shoulder.

I glared back. Mrs. Crocker and I had been having a perfectly nice conversation before Aunt Phyllis showed up. Why did she have to ruin everything?

I'll show her, I thought. *I'll make her see that I'm just as talented as Petunia.*

CHAPTER THIRTEEN

The Party

Violet was in a sour mood. For days she had been carrying on about what she was going to wear to the Dunsworth's party. Violet was upset that Petunia had been invited—she thought Petunia too young for a party. When it turned out that I was to attend as well, she was even more vexed. Her foul mood colored the atmosphere in the whole house and tried everyone's patience.

I, for one, wasn't even sure I wanted to go. What fun could I possibly have with Aunt Phyllis and Uncle Henry's friends? But nobody asked me what I thought.

Saturday finally arrived, and Violet's spirits lifted.

"I will not let your presence ruin my enjoyment of the party," she declared at breakfast, looking at Petunia and me. "If you are to attend, I will make the best of it."

She spent the entire afternoon at her dressing table, fixing her hair. Aldy and I spied on her and found it quite amusing. Meanwhile, Petunia was in a tizzy, trying to decide what to wear. My choice was easy, as I had but one party dress, the green one. Thankfully I had a hair ribbon that matched.

We boarded a cab as night was falling, and by the time we pulled up to the Dunsworth house—or should I say mansion—the streets were dark. But it was anything but dark at the

Dunsworth's. Torches had been lit at the gate, and lights blazed from every window. Two tall men stood guard at the door. They were dressed in armor, like ancient Roman gladiators, and grasped long spears. They even wore helmets. As we approached the door, the gladiators saluted.

Perhaps this will be fun, I thought.

Inside, a servant girl took Uncle Henry's top hat, and we stepped into a huge hall full of guests. An orchestra was playing on the far side of the room. The sound echoed off the high ceiling and swirled through the crowd, making it hard to hear Aunt Phyllis, who was issuing last-minute instructions. When she was done, she stepped forward, and a uniformed butler announced our arrival.

"Mr. and Mrs. Henry Leuts and family."

Immediately Aunt Phyllis plunged into the crowd, dragging Uncle Henry behind her and leaving Aldy, Violet, Petunia, and me on our own. While I stood there marveling at the size of the hall and the number of people, Petunia headed toward the orchestra, and Violet disappeared into the crowd.

"Let's eat," said Aldy, taking my arm.

He led me through several rooms. Everything looked as if it had been built for giants. The ceilings were enormously high, the doors tremendously tall, and the stone fireplaces so big you could have fit a grand piano inside each one. My shoes sank into the carpets.

Finally we entered the dining room. It looked like a wedding cake. The walls and ceiling were covered with carved fruit and flowers. I thought perhaps they were made of some kind of whipped cream, but Aldy said it was only plaster.

We approached a long buffet table. Aldy picked up a plate and piled it high with food—everything that would fit, and then some. I wasn't all that hungry. I was too busy eating with my eyes.

Aldy polished off his food in no time.

"That was tasty," he said, patting his stomach. "You sure you don't want any?"

"Maybe later," I said.

"Oh, good. I'll have some more later, too. C'mon, let's find out who else is here."

I followed him back to the main hall, past the orchestra, and into a parlor at the back of the house. It was full of children, and they were making a lot of noise. There were hundreds of tin soldiers in the middle of the floor, and the boys were shouting and banging the soldiers against each other. In a corner I spied Petunia, huddled with some girls from Miss Stipp's class. At the other end of the room, two boys were bouncing up and down on velvet couches. Aldy walked right up and said hello.

"Hi, Eli. Hi, Linden. This is my cousin, Penny."

"Hi," they said, and kept bouncing.

"Hi," I said.

Linden, the taller one, had green eyes with long eyelashes, and wavy hair the color of sand. He looked about my age. Eli was his younger brother. Eli's legs poked out of his knickers like twigs, and his black hair was cut so close to his head, it stuck straight up.

I sat down, and they stopped bouncing. We talked. Linden started telling jokes and making fun of himself. Every time a new girl walked into the room, Linden would poke Eli and say, "How 'bout that one? Is that the one for you?" and Eli would blush and murmur, "No," and Linden would giggle. I found myself giggling, too.

After a while a servant entered the room and banged on a gong. Everyone quieted down. The servant announced that the evening's entertainment was about to begin.

"Wait'll you see this," said Aldy.

"What?" I said.

"You'll see."

We joined a stream of people flowing into the garden. We crossed a large stone patio, edged with Grecian urns and dotted with tables and chairs. Beyond was a reflecting pool with a fountain of Venus and Cupid in the middle. Water spurted out of the fountain and sploshed into the pool. We passed a row of trees hung with little paper lanterns, from which candlelight flickered onto the surrounding lawn. We strolled down a pebbly path, past some high hedges, and finally reached a moonlit clearing.

"Look," said Aldy.

I looked.

There were three statues in the clearing, one male and two female. They were ancient Greek statues, with long, flowing togas, and sandals. They were so lifelike they seemed almost real.

"When does the entertainment begin?" I asked.

"It already has," he replied.

"What do you mean?"

"Look." He pointed at the statues.

I gasped. They were moving.

"They're people!" I cried. "With white makeup!"

"Shhhh!" said several guests.

A man appeared from behind a screen. He was dressed in a toga, too, but wore no makeup. He walked toward the crowd and began to speak.

The sun has set, the mists descend,
The moon's fair orb is veiled by cloud,
We mortals all do now pretend,
We voice the Ancient Truths aloud.
The chastest maiden will not blush,
To hear our verse arrayed in song,
And youth must bow to heaven's hush,
For hearts are broken 'ere too long.

I wasn't sure what it meant, but I liked the sound of it. I turned to Aldy.

"Hark, Aldebaran!" I said. "There are poets amongst us."

He giggled.

"I'm serious," I said.

"I know," he said, poking me in the ribs.

The poet began to stroll back and forth across the clearing, his voice rising and falling as if in song. Swaying with the rhythm of the words, he spoke about the love between a young man and a magical forest creature. The statues began to lean this way and that, as if blown by a gentle breeze. Then they began to dance, following the lead of one of the girls—skipping and running, jumping and twirling, joining hands in a circle and spinning round and round, their faces to the sky. I held my breath.

The lead girl broke the circle, and the others ran after her. They wove in and out of the hedges, disappearing in the darkness, then reappearing somewhere else. They reformed the circle, and the circle spun, faster and faster. The poet's words rushed and tumbled out of his mouth. The dancers leapt across the lawn. One came so close, I could hear her breathing and feel the rush of air as she passed. Behind the leaping dancers, the lanterns twinkled in the trees.

Finally the dancers slowed, and the words slowed, too. The dancers came to a stop and took new poses. The poet spoke a last verse, his voice deep and heavy. Then he fell silent.

The audience began to clap. I applauded wildly.

"Bravo! Bravo!" I shouted.

People turned to look at me.

I spied Aunt Phyllis making her way through the crowd in our direction, smiling at people around us as she pushed past them.

"Penelope," she hissed, as soon as she was within earshot. "It is not necessary to be quite so enthusiastic. Please act in a ladylike manner. We are in public."

"Oh, but it *is* necessary!" I exclaimed. "It was wonderful!"

"Aldebaran, why don't you take your cousin inside now? I believe the entertainment has ended."

"But I want to meet the actors!" I said.

"Not tonight," she said.

"But I do! I want to meet the actors!" I said, louder.

A lady standing next to me turned to see what the fuss was about. Aunt Phyllis saw her and changed her tone. "Perhaps another time, dear," she said, patting me on the arm and beaming a fake smile in the direction of the lady. "Come, let's go back to the house."

I could see that Aunt Phyllis meant business, so I didn't argue. She led the way, and Aldy and I followed her inside. I was shaking.

"Do you want to eat now?" asked Aldy.

"Eat? How can you think of eating at a time like this? I have never been so close to real live actors!" I felt as if I had a fever.

"They're just people, Penny."

"No, they're not just people," I insisted. "They're actors. Dancers. It's like make-believe, but it's real, but they're pretending at the same time. Weren't they wonderful? Wasn't it absolutely enchanting? Who are they? Have you seen them before? I want to meet them. Do you think we could meet them? Where do you think they're from?"

"I don't know," he said. "But if we're not going to eat, what do you want to do?"

"Do? Do? I don't know!" I said. "I just know I want to act. I want to act and dance like that. I want to be an actress!"

"Shhhh. Penny. Not so loud."

"What do you mean, not so loud?" I said, even louder.

"You know."

"No, I don't know, Aldy. I don't know. I honestly don't know how you put up with it."

"What are you talking about?"

"Everything. Your mother. Her rules. Your house. I just can't stand it."

He looked hurt. "But we have fun together."

"We do. But there's so much more! I know there is!"

"More what?"

"I don't know!"

I tore myself away and fled back to the garden. Beyond the patio, past the reflecting pool and the trees hung with lanterns, down the pebbly path by the high hedges. There were only a few people left in the clearing. The Greek statues were gathering their props and preparing to leave. I ran up to one of them. It was the lead girl.

"You were wonderful!" I gushed.

"Thank you, Princess Penelope," she said.

I gasped. "How do you know my name?"

"I am a Goddess," she declared.

"Yes, but—"

"Empress Isabelle, at your service," she said, bowing so low her head almost touched the ground.

"Isabelle!" I cried. "You! Here! How? I didn't recognize you in your white makeup!"

"We've formed a little troupe," she said, flipping a hand in the direction of the other actors. "My brothers and sister and me."

"That's wonderful," I said. I wanted to throw my arms around her. "You're so lucky. Where do you get your ideas, and how did you put that whole thing together?"

She smiled. "*I shot an arrow into the air.*"

"An arrow?"

"*I shot an arrow into the air.* And down fell our theatric."

"But how—"

"We seek Truth. Where Truth resides, we find Beauty, and in Beauty lies Art," she said with a grand sweep of her arm, as if that explained everything.

"But how did you come here, to the Dunsworth's?"

"I teach their daughters."

"Teach their daughters what?"

"Acting, of course."

"I thought you were a dancer."

"Acting, dancing, it's the same," she said, waving her hands around as she started down the path to the house.

"But where did you learn to dance?" I said, following.

"I was born by the sea," she said. "Why don't you come dance with me? We rehearse every Sunday morning in Golden Gate Park."

"Dance with you? How?"

She reached into her toga, pulled out a crumpled visiting card, and thrust it into my hand. "Here," she said.

She lifted her hem and made her way up the steps to the patio, but instead of going into the house, she turned toward a gate set into a hedge.

"Princess Penelope, I take my leave," she said. "Seek the stage in the bosom of your Soul." And with that, she disappeared through the gate.

I smoothed out the crumpled card.

"Isabelle Grey," it said. "Taylor and Geary Streets, San Francisco."

I squinted in the dim light. There was something else written at the bottom of the card.

In fancy letters it said, "Dancer and Actress Extraordinaire."

CHAPTER FOURTEEN

A Chance Encounter

During the dreary weeks that followed, Aunt Phyllis and I were constantly at odds.

"Sit up straight, Penelope."

"Speak only when spoken to, Penelope."

"Ladylike behavior, Penelope. *Ladylike behavior.*"

My hair was always in a tangle, my taste in music frightful, she didn't like my clothes. When I talked about acting or Shakespeare, she didn't want to hear. She even dared to broach the subject of my wearing a corset!

If she saw me reading, she would cluck like a nervous hen, "Tsk, tsk, tsk. You spend altogether too much time with your head in books, Penelope. You are going to ruin your eyes."

To make matters worse, Violet and Petunia were constantly picking on me. And I still hadn't heard a peep from the Prenderwinkels.

The only thing that gave me hope was the thought of Isabelle's acting troupe. If they rehearsed every Sunday in Golden Gate Park, perhaps I could convince Uncle Henry and Aunt Phyllis to take us on an outing.

Unfortunately, before I had a chance to bring up the subject, Aldy and Uncle Henry left on their hunting trip. I was stuck with Aunt Phyllis and the girls.

Be brave, Penelope, I told myself. *Like Mama. She was afraid of the ocean, and she went to sea anyway.*

Thinking of Mama, I resolved to accept my fate.

Then, one afternoon, I received a letter from Cassie.

Berkeley, July 28, 1889

Dear Penny,

Matilda had her puppies. Eight! When she saw them she licked them, their eyes were closed and they were ever so tiny. Like little squirmy rats! Now however they are five days old and are beginning to look like dogs. I wish you could see.

Your friend,

Cassie

Eight puppies! How I longed to hold them! How I longed to be rid of Violet and Petunia, to escape Aunt Phyllis and her House of Rules!

Alone in my room, I hugged Miranda, but still I felt miserable. I wanted to be brave, but it was hard to be brave when thinking about the puppies, and Aunt Phyllis, and having to go to school with Violet and Petunia in September, not to mention another month of comportment classes with the odious Miss Stipp. Worst of all, the summer was slipping away, and I wasn't any closer to becoming an actress.

Perhaps Shakespeare could raise my spirits.

I took my book down to the backyard and leafed through the pages. I loved looking at the pictures of famous actors and actresses—Ellen Terry in *Merry Wives of Windsor*, Violet Vanbrugh in *The Merchant of Venice*, Lillie Langtry in *Antony and Cleopatra*. I began to read some lines out loud from *The Tempest*.

All of a sudden I heard a man's voice.

"We are such stuff as dreams are made of."

"Hello?" I said.

"And our little life is rounded with a sleep."

"Who's there?" I said.

"'Tis I, Prospero, Duke of Milan."

I turned and saw a dashing, silver-haired gentleman peering at me over the hedge.

"Mr. Prenderwinkel?" I said.

"And whose acquaintance do I have the pleasure of making?" he asked in a deep, round voice.

"Penelope, sir. Penelope Leuts Bailey."

"Leuts? Rhymes with flutes?" Above his twinkly eyes was a set of very long eyebrows. They were long enough to twirl.

"Yes, sir."

"You're related to Master Aldebaran?"

"Yes, sir," I said. "First cousins."

"Cornelius Prenderwinkel," he said, clicking his heels and bowing a little bow. "At your service, mademoiselle."

I ran to the hedge and stuck out my hand. "How do you do? Did you get my note?"

"Your note?"

"I left it under your door."

"No. Perhaps the caretaker took it. We've been away on tour. Just returned late last night. Haven't seen the caretaker yet."

"I was just reading *The Tempest*. By Shakespeare."

"One of my most cherished roles."

"It is? You've acted in *The Tempest*? Have you been in many Shakespeare plays? Were you an actor your whole life? Are you famous? Have you been to Europe? Did you ever meet Sarah Bernhardt? Do you know a girl named Isabelle Grey?"

He laughed. "No, I've never made the acquaintance of the

celebrated Miss Bernhardt, nor do I know an Isabelle Grey. But yes, I've toured these thirty-eight states for many a year. And I've seen Weedon Grossmith and Vane Featherstone on the London stage. Even acted alongside Herbert Beerbohm Tree in *Herod*. This is my first San Francisco appearance in *The Tempest*. Should be a good one. We start rehearsals in two weeks. Open in October at the California Theatre. Bush Street."

"How do we get tickets? Can I come? I'm coming! I'll tell Aunt Phyllis this very evening! I'm sure she'll say yes when she finds out you're in it." My chest filled with pride. "Our very own neighbor."

"Come, by all means. Box office opens in a few weeks. Plenty of tickets, not to worry. Sixteen hundred seats."

I nearly burst with happiness. Then I had another thought. "Mr. Prenderwinkel?"

"My dear."

"May I ask you a question?"

"I believe you already have, my dear. Several."

"No, I mean a different question. How do you become an actor? Do you think I could be an actor?"

"An actor, eh?" Mr. Prenderwinkel stroked his chin. His silver hair glinted in the sunlight. "What makes you think you would like to be an actor?"

I hesitated. "It's . . . a feeling I get," I said. "I love to dance and sing, and everyone says I have a lovely voice, and . . ." I thought for a moment. "I like to pretend. I like to make believe I'm different people, like a pirate queen or a harem maiden or Cleopatra. And I like to show people I can do it."

"Hmm," said Mr. Prenderwinkel, looking at me closely. "So you want to act?"

I felt my cheeks getting hot.

"It's not an easy calling, my dear, not an easy calling. Very difficult, in fact. Have you discussed this with your parents?"

"Well, yes."

"And?"

"My father loves Shakespeare," I said. "And Gilbert and Sullivan, too."

"He approves, then?"

"It's what I've always wanted," I said, my cheeks getting even hotter. "Ever since I was little." I looked at the ground. "I don't think Papa would mind if I became an actress. He likes it when I sing. Mama says I'm to have elocution lessons if I behave while she's away." Then in a low voice I added, "It's only Aunt Phyllis who thinks theater isn't proper."

"Nothing to be ashamed of, my dear. Perfectly respectable art form, in my opinion. Threatening to some, I suppose. Still, one must do as one's heart dictates."

"Oh, do you truly think so?" I said, looking up. "Do you truly think there's hope?"

"Hope? Hope? There's always hope, my dear. Especially if you possess the courage to persevere in the face of opposition."

I wasn't sure what "persevere in the face of opposition" meant, but the fact that he thought that there was hope was enough to make me swoon. His words made me bold, and before I knew what I was saying, another question popped out of my mouth.

"Could I . . . perhaps you and your wife could tell me more about acting. Next week, perhaps? Before your rehearsals start for *The Tempest*?"

He thought for a moment. Then he said, "I'm afraid your aunt might not like that."

"She wouldn't have to know."

"Hmm. The plot thickens. Well, perhaps."

"How about tomorrow?"

"We'll be out."

"Monday, then?"

"So this would be a secret just between us actors, eh?"

"Yes, just between us," I said, nodding solemnly.

"Monday at three o'clock, then." He held out his hand for me to shake. "All the world's a stage."

"Exactly!" I said, pumping his hand up and down. "Thank you, Mr. Prenderwinkel, thank you! Just wait till I grow up and become a famous actress, you won't be sorry, I promise."

He gently withdrew his hand.

"You're welcome. And now, as the great bard once wrote, *'These our actors, as I foretold you, were all spirits, and are melted into air, into thin air.'* Farewell, my dear. Be brilliant."

"Good-bye. Don't forget, I want to learn more about acting! See you on Monday!"

I was so excited I thought I would burst, and there was no one with whom I could share my news. I grabbed my book and dashed to my room. I hugged Miranda and threw her up in the air and twirled her 'round and 'round.

"I'm going to learn about acting, Miranda! I'm going to be an actress! Just like Sarah Bernhardt and Isabelle Grey!"

CHAPTER FIFTEEN

School

July 7, 1889
Honolulu, Oahu, Kingdom of Hawaii

My dear Penelope,

By now your mother will have sailed, and I am anxious to see her. I hope you're settling in comfortably with Aunt Phyllis and Uncle Henry. Give Uncle Henry a clap on the back from me. Best not to do the same to Aunt Phyllis.

Our research is progressing satisfactorily save for the delay caused by Mr. Phroups's accident. We've been unable to identify any species of butterfly native to the Sandwich Islands beyond the two already known. One of those is named for King Kamehameha, rather a joke considering its small size, but the coloring is brilliant. All the other species seem to have been introduced by settlers, so the expedition is something of a disappointment to that part of me that hungers for new discoveries. There are, however, a profuse number of native plants that will be of interest to my colleagues in the botany department. We've been studying the activity of the butterflies in relation to some of these plants, particularly the process of pollination. I'll tell you more about it upon my return, my little butterfly, should you choose to indulge me.

Until then,

Papa

The envelope was postmarked July 11. Today was August 9. That meant it took four weeks for a boat to sail between Hawaii and San Francisco, which meant Mama had to be in Hawaii by now. Still, I worried about her safety. What did Papa mean when he wrote he was "anxious to see her"? Did he think she was in danger? How would we know if her boat was attacked by pirates? What if it sank in a storm?

I imagined the newspaper headline:

MOTHER LEAVES CHILD IN SAN FRANCISCO,
IS LOST AT SEA

I wondered if Papa knew that Aunt Phyllis thought the theater was sinful. What would he think of Isabelle Grey, and Mr. Prenderwinkel, and my plan to become an actress? I liked to think that Papa would approve, but in truth I didn't know, despite what I had told Mr. Prenderwinkel. My plan to become an actress had grown a great deal since Papa had left for the islands. After seeing Isabelle and her troupe I was sure, surer than I'd ever been of anything in my whole life, that I was meant to be an actress. And when I talked to the Prenderwinkels on Monday, I was going to find out how.

The next day I awoke with a fever. Aunt Phyllis was alarmed and sent for the doctor. He felt my forehead and poked my belly, looked down my throat and squeezed my neck. He said to keep the other children away from me, prescribed a cold bath, and said, "I'll be back."

After the bath I crawled into bed. The light hurt my eyes, so Winifred drew the curtains and left me alone in the dark room. I huddled under the covers, feverish and miserable. Everything ached.

For a whole week I was ill. The doctor gave me some horrible medicine that tasted like Crocker's Digestive Syrup. After I took it, he felt my forehead and said there was nothing to do but to wait till the fever broke. Mrs. Campbell sent up cold compresses and chamomile tea.

Nights were the worst. I tossed and turned, wishing I was home in Berkeley with Mama by my side. I dreamed I was on a stage in front of a huge audience, and when I opened my mouth to speak, nothing came out. I dreamed I was standing on the deck of a ship at sea and a ferocious storm blew up. The ship rolled and heaved. Monstrous waves crashed across the bow, and I was swept overboard. I cried out in fear and woke myself up.

Finally the fever broke, and I felt much improved. Mrs. Campbell sent up toast and custard—she said the custard would help me regain my strength. Wrapped in Mama's shawl, I read my Shakespeare and watched the clouds through the window. Then Aunt Phyllis ordered Winifred to change the sheets, and she took away the shawl for washing. She even took away Miranda. When I protested, Aunt Phyllis said, "Stop fussing. You are too old for dolls."

My spirits sank. I had missed my meeting with Mr. and Mrs. Prenderwinkel. Would I ever be an actress? I couldn't bear to wait until Mama and Papa returned.

People run away to join the circus. I will run away to join the theater.

But running away is no lark. One needs a plan.

Where would I go? Who would take me in? What if I got caught? What would Mama and Papa say when they returned? If they returned?

I will never be an actress as long as I am stuck under Aunt Phyllis's thumb.

As soon as I was up and about, I began to frequent the backyard. With weak and wobbly legs I climbed the pirate ship and peered over the hedge, searching for Mr. and Mrs.

Prenderwinkel. I spied their table and chairs, their rose bushes and fig tree, but I never spied them. Their garden lay empty, and I was alone.

A few days later Aunt Phyllis began to make rumblings about Uncle Henry's return. It seemed the hunting trip would soon be over. Perhaps when they got back, we'd be able to take that outing to Golden Gate Park, find Isabelle's troupe, and watch them rehearse. School would be starting shortly, too. I dreaded having to go to school with Violet and Petunia, yet I took some comfort in the thought that Aldy might be in my class, since he was my age. I hoped Consuela would be in my class, too.

At one of our last classes with Miss Stipp, I asked Consuela about school. She said there was a good chance we'd have the same teacher, because there were only two classes in each grade. She and Aldy were in Miss Adelaide's class, and Miss Adelaide was very sympathetic. The other sixth grade teacher, Mr. Thaddeus Ducree, was a mean man with long whiskers, which he chewed on when he was angry. I couldn't find out anything more, because Miss Stipp told us to stop prattling.

As the first day of school approached, Aunt Phyllis became even more fussy and demanding.

"There is so much to do!" she exclaimed. "School supplies to be bought. Shoes! Gloves! Hats! Girls. Girls!"

On our morning constitutionals she herded us from shop to shop. We paid a visit to Mrs. Plumbottom, where Violet and Petunia were fitted for new dresses. I didn't have to ask if there would be a new dress for me. I already knew the answer. My wardrobe would have to do until Mama and Papa got home.

Before the week was out, Aldy and Uncle Henry returned. There was a hustle and a bustle as they unloaded their gear— tents and blankets, fishing poles and rifles, lanterns and cook pots, gear boxes and trunks. Uncle Henry pronounced the expedition a great success and boasted of Aldy's "prowess" with the fishing rod. The big surprise was that Uncle Henry had grown a beard. And it was red! Aldy's hair was overgrown, too, and both of them smelled terrible. Aunt Phyllis wrinkled her nose and sent Aldy straight to the bathtub.

After his bath, Aldy was eager to talk about his adventures.

"We caught so many fish that Father's friends said I was a regular good-luck charm," he said.

"Oh," I said.

"Our guide taught me how to gut 'em. First you cut out all the intestines, 'cause they make you sick. Then you fry 'em up good—the fish, not the intestines. Heads and all. Even the slimy eyeballs."

I pictured a slimy eyeball staring up at me from a plate. "Did you eat the eyeballs?"

"Oh, yeah," he said. "They're the best part."

"No!" I gasped.

He looked at me like I was thick in the head. "You don't eat eyeballs, Penny."

"Oh," I said.

"We had fish every day when we weren't having squirrel or rabbit or something," he continued.

"You ate a rabbit?"

"Yes, but mostly we ate so much fish I don't ever want to see a fish again."

"Me, too. I hate fish."

"And I learned how to shoot. With a real rifle."

"You didn't kill anything, did you?"

"Almost. Well, not exactly. But I came close. Real close."

"I'm glad you didn't kill anything," I said.

"And we saw Indians."

"Indians! Real live Indians? Did you talk to them? What did they look like? Did they have Indian children? What did they say?"

"I dunno," he shrugged. "They were wearing clothes, just like anybody else. We didn't actually talk to them. We just saw them. In the trading store, when we made a trip into town for provisions."

"Oh," I said. "But if you didn't talk to them how did you know they were Indians?"

"They were talking Indian," he said.

There was a silence.

"Father says I'm more of a man now."

"Why?"

"Because I'm learning to do man things. Things you prob'ly don't know about. 'Cause you're a girl and all. No offense."

"Oh," I said.

"I feel like a man, too."

"Oh," I said. "Do you want to play outside?"

"Play what? Pirates?"

"All right," I said.

"Nah. Men don't play pirates."

"Oh? What do men play?"

"I dunno. I suppose they hunt and fish and smoke cigars. Like this."

He pretended to smoke a cigar. I laughed.

"You silly goose!" I said, poking him.

But Aldy didn't laugh. "I'm serious!" he said.

"I can see you're serious," I snapped. "I can see you take yourself very seriously. Why don't you go play with some other men? Why don't you go eat some slimy eyeballs?" I stalked out of the room.

"Penny!" he called after me. "Come on. I'll play pirates."

"I lost my flavor for pirates!" I yelled.

Later I was sorry. I went to his room to apologize, but he didn't want to talk.

"Go away," he said. "I'm recovering from my hunting trip."

The day before school started, a letter arrived from Mama.

July 5, 1889
On board the Providence

Dearest Penelope,

*We are only three days out from San Francisco and already I
am wondering whether I made a mistake in leaving you behind. I
miss you, and am saddened when I think of our empty house in
Berkeley, and my empty painting studio.*

*I was sickly and a bit frightened the first day or two but now I
have gotten my sea legs and it is better, after all, to be on deck
enjoying the fresh air than lying below in the cabin, where the air
is close. I share the cabin with a young lady who is going to Hawaii
to marry a missionary. We have become friends. We stroll the deck
when the weather is fair, and she lets me sketch her. When the
breeze shifts, the sailors leap into action, and we must lift our skirts
and jump out of their way.*

*Our voyage will take between three and five weeks, depending
on whether or not we get favorable winds. I hope it will be three
weeks and not five, as I haven't, as yet, completely conquered my
fear of the water. When I look out over the side of the ship, the
blue-green sea seems very deep, indeed.*

*I hope you are behaving and not giving Aunt and Uncle too
much trouble. Last night we had a special Fourth of July dinner,
followed by a small fireworks display off the stern. It was the first
Independence Day I have not celebrated with you, and I shed some
tears.*

Be well, my sweet. I shall write again soon.

Love,

Mama

That night, before I got into bed, I laid out my clothes and checked my rucksack to make sure I had everything I needed for school. I rearranged my new notebook, pencils, and eraser a thousand times. Winifred had been kind enough to return Miranda, and I tucked her into bed with an extra prayer.

Please, Lord, give me Miss Adelaide so I can be in the same class as Consuela and Aldy. May Miss Adelaide be kind, and may she like the theater. And if You don't see fit to give me Miss Adelaide, please make Mr. Ducree not as mean as they say. But he can keep chewing on his whiskers if he wants to.

I got into bed but couldn't fall asleep. I lay on my back. I lay on my belly. I flopped from one side to the other. What would the new school be like? I must have stayed awake half the night, and when I finally fell asleep, I slept fitfully.

At the crack of dawn my eyes flew open. I washed and dressed with a fluttering stomach, and at breakfast I couldn't eat a thing. When it was time to go, Aunt Phyllis lined us up at the door, looked us up and down, and handed each of us a lunch.

"Penelope, calico is a bit informal for school, don't you think?"

"No," I said.

Consuela and I had agreed to wear our calico skirts on the first day.

Aunt Phyllis pursed her lips. Then she sniffed and said, "I suppose it will do."

"It'll do for people from Berkeley who don't know any better," said Petunia under her breath.

Aldy pinched Petunia's behind. She slapped his arm.

"Children!" Aunt Phyllis said. She straightened her back, lifted her chin, and cleared her throat. "Eh-hrm. Your father and I expect you to distinguish yourselves at school this year. The three of you represent the finest flowering of the Leuts family tree." She paused and looked down her nose. "Hr-hm. Penelope, you too."

"We expect all of you, at all times, to display such manners as reflect the very finest breeding. Your teachers expect obedience and respect, and so do we." She shook her head slightly. A small sigh escaped her lips. "For better or worse, our reputation is in your hands. Uphold our good name, and you will make us proud."

After her speech she put on her hat and gloves and picked up her parasol. "Let us go," she said. "Papers must be filled out for Penelope."

We set out for school, Aunt Phyllis in the lead. It was a walk of some ten blocks. I stuck close to Aldy and kept my distance from the girls.

My head was filled with questions. What if the teacher didn't like me? What if I didn't like the teacher? What if the girls were uppity? What if the boys were mean?

We rounded a corner, and the school came into view. It was the biggest school I'd ever seen, with dark-brown bricks, small windows, and little towers that made it look like a fortress—forbidding and cold.

"Aldy, you will come with us to the office," said Aunt Phyllis. "Then you can show Penny to the sixth grade rooms." She nodded to Petunia and Violet. "All right, girls, off with you. And remember, make us proud. Penelope, this way."

Petunia headed in one direction, Violet in another. Aldy and I followed Aunt Phyllis down a long, dark corridor. The floor smelled of fresh wax. Mothers and children milled about. The corridor twisted and turned. I couldn't keep track of where we were going, and I wondered if I would ever find my way in this big school, where every corridor looked the same.

"Didn't we walk down this hall already?" I asked Aldy as we turned another corner.

"No," he said.

Finally we reached the office. Aunt Phyllis introduced me to

Miss Tumleigh, the principal. Miss Tumleigh gave Aunt Phyllis some papers to fill out. I was so nervous about which teacher I would get that I almost forgot to breathe. Would it be Miss Adelaide? Or would I be stuck with the dreaded Mr. Thaddeus Ducree?

CHAPTER SIXTEEN

A Grand Idea

I held my breath as Miss Tumleigh looked over the papers. She tapped a pencil on the counter as she read. *Tap tap tap tap.* Finally she handed the papers to her clerk and said, "Please add Penelope to Mr. Ducree's roll."

Oh no! My mouth fell open. I looked at Aldy. He was horrified, too.

"You had asked me to remind you that Miss Adelaide is short of girls," said the clerk.

Miss Tumleigh nodded. "Hmm," she said.

I placed a hand on Aldy's arm.

"All right," said Miss Tumleigh. "Put her with Miss Adelaide, then."

I was so happy I almost danced a jig. Fortune had smiled upon me.

Aunt Phyllis bid us good-bye, and I startled her with a peck on the cheek. She drew back in surprise. From the look on her face I judged she was about to say something, but she held her tongue. Then she adjusted the feather on her hat and left.

I followed Aldy down the hall. On the way I wondered if school was starting today in Berkeley. I missed it all so much— my friends, and Miss Barker, and the swings in the yard, and the tall eucalyptus trees that grew all around, and Cassie, who played with me every day after school and who could sit with me for hours in the shade of the eucalyptus tree, talking about what it would be like to be an actress, and—

"And you are?"

"Aldebaran Leuts," said Aldy to a young woman who was standing in front of a classroom.

"Leuts . . . Hmm," she said, running a finger down a notebook. She wore thick, gold-rimmed spectacles, but they must not have worked, for she held the notebook right up to her nose as if she couldn't see. Her thick, chestnut hair was parted in the middle and tamed into a low bun. Two little curls dangled over her forehead.

When she found Aldy's name, she checked it off in her notebook. "How do you do, Aldebaran?" she said with a smile, shaking his hand. "I'm Miss Adelaide." She turned to me. "And you are?"

"Penelope Leuts Bailey," I said.

She looked in her notebook. The two little curls danced in the air. When she looked up, there was a question mark in her eyes.

"There must be some mistake. You're not on my list."

"I'm new," I said. "Miss Tumleigh said to report to you."

"All right, I'll check with Miss Tumleigh later. Welcome, Penelope." She put out her hand. "How do you do?" she said, in a voice that sounded like she truly wanted to know.

"Fine, thank you," I said, smiling.

She smiled back. She had a nice smile. It made me bold. "Would you call me by my nickname, please?" I said. "Penny?"

"Me, too," said Aldy.

She looked at Aldy. "You want me to call you Penny?" she said.

"N . . . no," he stammered, "I mean, I like Penny better than Penelope. I mean . . ." He blushed. "You can call me Aldy."

"Forgive me, Aldy, I was teasing," she said. "Why don't you go inside and take your seats?"

We walked in and sat down. A few children were already

there, laughing and scuttling back and forth between the wooden desks. I recognized two girls from comportment class. They sat next to each other, talking quietly, their hands folded in their laps, prim in their starched dresses.

Consuela wasn't there yet, but Linden was. I was surprised. I had assumed he was older than sixth grade because he was so tall. Soon the seats were almost full, and Consuela still hadn't arrived. The bell rang. Miss Adelaide came in from the hall. As soon as she shut the door behind her, it flew open.

"Is this Miss Adelaide's class?" said Consuela, breathlessly. "Sorry I'm late. My mother—"

"It's all right, dear," said Miss Adelaide. "Take a seat, please."

I waved at Consuela, and she sat down next to me. She was wearing her calico skirt, just as we had agreed.

"Hi!" she whispered. "My mother never gets me anywhere on time."

"I was assigned to Miss Adelaide!" I said.

"I know!" she said.

"We'll be able to pass notes."

Miss Adelaide cleared her throat. The room fell quiet.

"Good morning, children."

"Good morning, Miss Adelaide," said the class.

"Welcome to Class Six-A. I am Miss Adelaide." She spelled her name on the blackboard. "Any questions? Yes, in the last row. Tell me your name, dear."

"Virginia," said a voice. "May I change seats, please? I can't see."

I turned around. Virginia was very short.

Miss Adelaide smiled. "Of course. Why don't you switch seats with . . ." She looked around. "With this gentleman in the front row? And you are?"

"Linden James," said Linden, standing.

He took his rucksack and walked up the row. I smiled at him as he went by. He nodded and plopped down in the seat behind me.

"We will be working very hard this year, children. It's time for you to become serious scholars, and I have high expectations for everyone. We'll be studying geography, civics, history, Latin, and penmanship. And, of course, reading, composition, and mathematics, in which I trust you will all make excellent progress. Also, nature study three times a week, physical culture every Monday and Thursday, and music on Wednesdays."

Miss Adelaide looked at the names in her notebook.

"Theodosia and Jacob, would you please come to the front of the room and help me distribute books?"

Theodosia, one of the girls from Miss Stipp's class, joined the boy named Jacob at the front of the room. As they handed out books, Miss Adelaide explained the class routines and something she called "the circle of chores." The circle of chores meant that each week we were assigned different tasks like carrying out the trash, sweeping the floor, or washing the blackboard. She said the circle of chores was very important because it would teach us that we were all dependent on each other and everyone was responsible for the well-being of the classroom. I knew all about chores and didn't hold a very high opinion of them, but I thought I wouldn't much mind being part of a circle of chores as long as I had a teacher as sympathetic as Miss Adelaide.

The morning passed swiftly. After lunch we were sent outside with Mr. Ducree's class and the two fifth grade classes. The boys played tag. I wanted to play, too, but Aunt Phyllis's words kept ringing in my ears. "Ladylike behavior, Penelope. *Ladylike behavior.*" I didn't want to make a poor impression on my first day of school. So I sat and chatted with Consuela.

"I think he's quite handsome, don't you?" said Consuela.

"Who?" I said.

"The boy who sits behind you. Linden."

I watched Linden as he tagged Aldy. "Are you soft on Linden?" I said, leaning closer.

"No," she said. "Are you?"

"No. But he is quite handsome. And funny. He makes me laugh."

"Do you know him?"

"We met over the summer," I said. "Consuela? I have an idea."

"What?"

"Don't you think Linden would make a splendid Romeo? Let's ask Miss Adelaide if we can stage a scene from *Romeo and Juliet!*"

"Do you think she'd let us?"

"It'd be scrumptious!"

"What a perfect idea!"

"Absolutely perfect."

Despite a lesson in Latin grammar, the afternoon flew by. At the end of the day, Consuela and I approached Miss Adelaide. We agreed that I would do the asking, since it had been my idea.

"Miss Adelaide, may we speak to you for a moment, please?" I asked.

"Certainly."

"Um. . . We were thinking . . . um . . ."

"A dangerous activity," she said.

"What?"

"Thinking," she said. "A dangerous activity."

I ignored her, even though I knew she was trying to be funny. "We were thinking that perhaps we could do some dramatical study. In class."

"Dramatical study?"

"Like Shakespeare. Perhaps we could do some Shakespeare." Saying Shakespeare's name gave me confidence. I took a deep breath. "I've been reading Shakespeare over the summer, and back in my school in Berkeley, Miss Barker said we should practice our elocution over the summer because sixth grade is the perfect time to begin Shakespeare. So I've been studying *Romeo and Juliet* and I've got Juliet's speeches pretty near memorized, but perhaps instead of just reciting Shakespeare we could act it out on a stage."

I took another deep breath and waited. Miss Adelaide smiled her beautiful smile.

"Interesting idea, Penny," she said.

"Do you think so? Would it be possible? Because, you see, I want to be an actress when I grow up, like Sarah Bernhardt and Isabelle Grey and Cornelius Prenderwinkel, and I'm sure Mr. Prenderwinkel would say Shakespeare is the perfect place to start. He's our neighbor, and he's a real Shakespearean actor who's toured all over the world, and he's to appear in *The Tempest* soon at the California Theatre and Aunt Phyllis says we might buy tickets"—this last was a fib, but I couldn't help myself—"so perhaps we could start right here in your class with *Romeo and Juliet*."

Behind her thick spectacles, Miss Adelaide's eyes widened. Then she said, "Well, the sixth grade curriculum does call for recitations of poetry. But *Romeo and Juliet*—I don't know. Perhaps we could begin with some poems by Shakespeare. He wrote a good many sonnets, you know."

"Oh, anything by Shakespeare would be magnificent!" I said. "Anything at all." I put a hand to my chest. I was quite overcome. "Thank you, Miss Adelaide!" I said. "May I shake your hand?" And before she could reply, I seized her hand and squeezed it.

"As for your playacting idea, I'll discuss it with Miss Tumleigh," she said, removing her hand from my squeeze. "And then we'll see. It might be a few weeks before you hear. Miss Tumleigh is very busy right now."

"Oh, thank you, Miss Adelaide," I said.

"Thank you, Miss Adelaide," said Consuela.

Consuela and I rushed into the hall. We clasped hands and hopped a little hop.

"She'll do it, I know she will!" I exclaimed. "Oh, Consuela, perhaps I'll be an actress someday after all!"

CHAPTER SEVENTEEN

A Wish Comes True

All through September, I waited for an answer from Miss Adelaide. In the meantime I kept a lookout for Mr. Prenderwinkel, but he was never home. I despaired of ever seeing him again. Then one day I saw an advertisement for *The Tempest* in Uncle Henry's newspaper, right next to the one for Lotta Crabtree, the famous variety star. "Tickets selling fast," it said. I ran straight to Aunt Phyllis.

"Do you think we might go to see Mr. Prenderwinkel in *The Tempest*?"

"Certainly not," she said. "I disapprove thoroughly of your interest in the theater."

"But Aunt Phyllis—"

"I refuse to participate in this . . . this obsession."

"But Mr. Prenderwinkel said—"

"It's bad enough that a vaudevillian should be living next door," she said. "But to think that he could influence an impressionable child is simply scandalous."

"But it's Shakespeare," I said. "It's the greatest book in the English language."

"The greatest book in the English language," she said, "is neither a play, nor a novel, nor a poem. It is the Holy Bible. And it would behoove you to spend more time reading it, rather than filling your head with the aforementioned frivolities. Now if you will excuse me, I must take Petunia to her violin lesson at the conservatory."

I held my tongue, as it would have done no good to object. I fled to my room, held Miranda to my chest, and cried.

I was perched on the pirate ship one afternoon in October, reading a book by Mr. Charles Dickens, when I heard voices in the garden next door. I jumped off the ship and scurried over to the hedge. Mr. Prenderwinkel and his wife were just sitting down at the table. Mrs. Prenderwinkel was holding an open newspaper, from which she was reading aloud.

"'It is insufficient to say that Mr. Cornelius Prenderwinkel *acts* the role of Prospero; he lives it, nay, he *is* Prospero! One could almost imagine the part had been written for him, so admirably does he fill it.'" Her voice tinkled like a bell.

Mr. Prenderwinkel chuckled.

"Listen, there's more," said Mrs. Prenderwinkel. "'The entire cast acquits itself admirably in this lively new production. We can only surmise that the remainder of the run will be standing room only.'"

Mrs. Prenderwinkel put down the paper. "Isn't that gratifying?" she said.

"Very gratifying, my dear," he said, leaning back in his chair and crossing his arms. "Would you mind reading that part about the opening scene once more?"

"Not at all," she said. "Let's see. . . . Here it is. 'Cornelius Prenderwinkel's performance as Prospero was a triumph. From his opening dialogue with Miranda to the closing lines of the Epilogue, the old master dazzles with a depth of skill that has scarcely been seen in San Francisco in recent years.'"

Mr. Prenderwinkel chuckled. "The old master, eh?" Then he sighed a deep sigh. "Thank you, my dear."

"It warms my heart to hear them praise your acting," she said, "for you've worked so hard and endured so much. And at your age! Why, it makes me want to weep."

Her shoulders began to shake, and he rose and put an arm around her. I began to think that perhaps I shouldn't be peeping at them over the hedge. I was about to draw back when the bush I was leaning on gave way, and I fell in a heap into their garden.

"Well, well, if it isn't our little aspiring thespian," said Mr. Prenderwinkel. "Darling, we have an audience."

"Oh!" I said, my face getting hot. "Please excuse me. I . . . I shouldn't have spied on you. I know it's bad manners, but I just now heard your voices, and was that the review of *The Tempest* that Mrs. Prenderwinkel was reading? What does it feel like to have your name in the paper? And what's an aspiring thespian?"

"An aspiring thespian is someone who wants to be an actor," said Mr. Prenderwinkel. "Like you."

"Won't you come closer?" said Mrs. Prenderwinkel. "I don't believe we've met."

"Penelope Leuts Bailey," I said, brushing off my skirt. "But my friends call me Penny." Seized by a sudden impulse, I curtsied. I don't know why. I never curtsy.

"Lovely to meet you, Penny," she said. "I'm Abigail Sloane."

"Oh. I thought you were Mrs. Prenderwinkel."

"I am. Sloane is my stage name."

"I didn't know you could have a stage name!"

"Yes," she said, dabbing at her eyes with a handkerchief. "Don't mind my tears, darling. My emotions are rather . . . fluid. Actresses tend to be that way."

"What way?" I said.

"You know. Transparent," she said. "As if you can see through their feelings."

My eyes grew wide. She was describing exactly how I sometimes felt.

"Splendid review, eh?" said Mr. Prenderwinkel.

"Oh, yes," I said. "But I am completely crushed."

"Crushed?" said Mrs. Prenderwinkel. "Why?"

"Because Aunt Phyllis won't let me see your play."

"Oh, poor dear," she said. "What a shame."

"It's worse than a shame," I said. "It's a catastrophe. How will I ever become an actress if I'm not allowed to see any plays?"

Mr. Prenderwinkel shook his head. "Too bad your aunt is so narrow-minded."

"Well," I said. "She's certainly not the easiest of aunts. I don't know how I will stand it till Christmas. It'll be months before Mama and Papa come back. *If* they come back. If they aren't attacked by pirates."

"Pirates?" they both said.

"They've gone to Hawaii to study dead butterflies," I said. "It's a very long way from here. And Mrs. Campbell says there are pirates in the South Seas. And storms and hurricanes and ty-poons."

"Indeed," said Mr. Prenderwinkel.

"Typhoons," said Mrs. Prenderwinkel.

"Do you think they'll be all right?" I asked.

"Of course they will," said Mrs. Prenderwinkel.

"No doubt about it," said Mr. Prenderwinkel.

"I hope so," I said. "Because all of this worrying is giving me a headache. And I don't know how long I can stand Aunt Phyllis."

"Courage, my dear," said Mr. Prenderwinkel.

I sighed. "At least I like Miss Adelaide. My teacher. And my friend Consuela Hopkins is in my class. And if I'm truly, truly lucky, Miss Adelaide will let us have a recitation of poetry and perhaps perform some scenes from a play. I told her we should try *Romeo and Juliet*. With me as Juliet, of course. Wouldn't that be splendid?"

"It would be glorious, my little morning glory," said Mr. Prenderwinkel.

"May your wish come true," said Mrs. Prenderwinkel.

"Amen," I said.

True to Miss Adelaide's promise, within a few weeks we were reciting poetry in class. Miss Adelaide believed firmly in elocution and praised mine to the hilt.

"Men *and women*," she said, "must be prepared to speak in public. Girls, you must learn to form your opinions and express them well, for someday women may be given the right to vote. We live in the Age of Progress, after all."

Some of the girls started to whisper. I knew Aunt Phyllis wouldn't approve of what Miss Adelaide was saying, but Mama would. Mama believes in woman suffrage. She wants to be able to vote.

"In four months we'll be living in the 1890s," Miss Adelaide went on. "By the time you are adults, it will be the twentieth century. Imagine! The population of the United States is now over fifty million!" Miss Adelaide's eyes sparkled.

I slipped a note to Consuela. "Imagine!" it said.

Consuela grinned. *Imagine* was Miss Adelaide's favorite word.

As the weeks went by, everyone in the class grew to love Miss Adelaide. Sometimes Consuela and I laughed at the things the boys said, for all of them were smitten.

"May I hold the door for you, Miss Adelaide?"

"Do you need that note taken to the principal, Miss Adelaide?"

"That dress is very becoming, Miss Adelaide."

This last was spoken by Linden, who was quite bold. The other boys teased him for being so forward as to pay a compliment to the teacher, but I think they were jealous. I thought Linden was brave to say such a thing in public.

During the second week of October, Miss Adelaide made an announcement.

"I have spoken to Miss Tumleigh," she said, "and she has agreed to let our class stage a performance."

"Oh!" I cried.

Everyone turned around in their seats to look at me.

Miss Adelaide continued. "Penny and Consuela have been asking since school began if we could perform some scenes from Shakespeare."

I could feel my ears getting hot.

". . . and as Shakespeare is normally a part of the sixth grade curriculum, Miss Tumleigh and I have decided that it would be an appropriate choice."

I almost jumped out of my seat. Consuela reached over and grabbed my hand.

"Penny and Consuela, would you please come to the front of the room and help me distribute these books? For the next several weeks we will be reading scenes and poems aloud in class. Anyone who would like to participate may audition with a partner. If you would like to recite a poem, you will find the poems at the back of the book in the section labeled "One Hundred and Fifty-Four Sonnets." Or you may choose to read a scene from *Romeo and Juliet*. The audition will be two weeks from today, on October twenty fifth. We will have six weeks of rehearsal and then two performances on Thursday, December 5—one for the upper school in the afternoon, and one for friends and family in the evening."

Consuela and I handed out the books while Miss Adelaide wrote a letter about the play on the blackboard.

"Would everyone please copy this permission slip?" said Miss Adelaide. "Your best handwriting, please. Remember, these will be read by your parents."

—⁓—

Dear Sir and Madam,

*The children of Class 6-A will be performing excerpts from
Shakespeare at 7:30 p.m. on the evening of Thursday, December 5
in the school auditorium. Please sign and return the form below if
you agree to let your child participate.*

My heart sank. If only my parents were here to sign the per-
mission slip. But they weren't. They were far away in Hawaii.
My permission slip would be read by Aunt Phyllis and Uncle
Henry. And I already knew what Aunt Phyllis would say.

CHAPTER EIGHTEEN

Isabelle in the Park

She read the permission slip and looked at me as if I had gone completely mad.

"Absolutely not," she said.

"But Aunt Phyllis—"

"Don't interrupt, Penelope. I forbid you to perform in public, and that's final."

"But you let me perform in your musicale. And you're letting Petunia study at the music conservatory."

She looked flustered. "This . . . this is entirely different. The musicale was in the privacy of our own home. This is a public event."

"But I don't see—"

"Music is not the same as acting," she said pulling herself even more erect than usual. "Petunia does not intend to become a professional. The study of music cultivates the higher senses; it is uplifting. Acting, on the other hand, is entirely unwholesome. Everyone knows that actresses are lascivious. They are celebrated for their immodest behavior. The idea of your taking the stage in public is abhorrent. Simply abhorrent."

"But you don't understand."

"Do not contradict me, Penelope, I understand perfectly. I understand that young girls should be modest and demure and not seek attention. I understand that you have always been something of a showoff and that the last thing you need is encouragement. What could that teacher of yours be thinking? Does she think I am raising another Lotta Crabtree? I've half a mind to switch you to Mr. Ducree's class."

"Oh, no!" I said. "Don't do that."

"Hrmph," she said.

Tears sprang to my eyes. "I'll be modest. I promise. But please don't switch me out of Miss Adelaide's."

"Stop whining."

"But I want to act!"

"Enough!" She crumpled the permission slip and let it drop to the floor.

"Mama would let me," I said, under my breath.

She didn't hear me. "At least your teacher has the sense to know that some parents don't approve of their daughters gallivanting about in public, in front of an audience. And in a love scene! It's scandalous. I've half a mind to talk to Miss Tumleigh."

"That won't be necessary," I said.

She narrowed her eyes. "Very well. Please inform Miss Adelaide of my decision. You may be excused."

I snatched the permission slip off the floor and stuffed it into my pocket. Then I stomped up to my room and slammed the door.

I don't care what she thinks. I am going to be in this play.

I had finally convinced Uncle Henry and Aunt Phyllis to take us on an outing to Golden Gate Park. Aunt Phyllis didn't want to go, but Uncle Henry said that as it was the last weekend in October, we should all take advantage of the good weather before the rainy season began.

When we reached the park, the sun was out, and a gentle breeze was blowing. Aunt Phyllis and Uncle Henry settled themselves on a bench. I wanted to look for Isabelle right away.

"Do you mind if Aldy and I take a walk?" I asked.

"Go ahead," said Uncle Henry.

"But don't stray too far," said Aunt Phyllis.

In the distance we saw some boys playing ball. Aldy pulled me in their direction. It turned out to be Linden, his brother Eli, and Horace, a boy in Miss Adelaide's class who was something of a bully.

"Hey, Aldy, wanna play?" asked Horace, with a lopsided grin.

"Sure," said Aldy. He looked at me out of the corner of his eye. "Can Penny play, too?"

"That's okay," I said, "I have to go look for someone."

"Hey Aldy, what'ja doin' with a redhead? Is she your *girl-friend*?" said Horace, loud enough for half the park to hear.

"No," said Aldy. "She's not my friend. She's only my cousin." He ran toward Linden, holding his hands up so Horace would throw him the ball.

Not his friend? What does he mean, ONLY his cousin?

"Did'ja tell her girls can't play?" yelled Horace.

Aldy didn't answer. He caught the ball and kept running. He didn't even look at me.

I'm good at ball. He knows it, too.

Aldy threw the ball to Eli. Eli looked around, then threw it to Linden. Linden turned on a dime and threw it back to Horace. It whizzed past me. I jumped to catch it, but it was too high. Horace threw to Aldy. Aldy looked at me as if he were going to throw it to me, but instead he looked from boy to boy to boy and threw it back to Eli.

I could feel my face turning red. I walked away and plopped down on a bench. I had half a mind to cry, just to make Aldy feel bad. I dug the toe of my shoe in the dirt.

Ugly, brown shoes. Why doesn't Mama have better sense than to buy me such ugly shoes?

Then I remembered Isabelle. I jumped up and continued my search, following a path that curved through the trees. Little speckled birds scurried along the ground in front of me, their feathered crowns bobbing and bouncing. Now and then I caught a glimpse of boats on a distant lake. I hadn't realized the park was so big. How would I ever find Isabelle?

Just as I was beginning to get discouraged, I rounded a bend, and lo and behold, there she was.

"Isabelle!" I cried. "I was hoping to find you!"

She was wearing a long purple gown, pleated and tied in the Grecian style. She turned to her companions. "Everyone, this is Penelope. Penelope, these are my older brothers, Raymond and Arthur, and my older sister, Elizabeth."

"Your troupe!"

"Greetings, Penelope," said Raymond. "Would you care to dance?"

"Stop it, Ray," said Elizabeth, poking her brother. She smiled at me. "I'm Bets."

I straightened my skirts. "How do you do?"

Bets was tall, like Isabelle, and her light brown hair was turned up in a smart style.

Raymond held out his hand. "Raymond Grey."

I reached out to shake his hand, but he flipped mine over and kissed it. I giggled.

Raymond was the one who had recited poetry at the Dunsworth's party. He was older than Isabelle—in his twenties, I guessed—but he didn't look like a regular grownup. He had wild, brown eyes and a long, bushy beard, and his dark hair seemed to sprout in all directions from the top of his head.

"And I'm Artie," said the other brother. He was taller and fairer than Raymond, but with the same wild eyes. He reminded me of Papa's university students.

"I've been thinking about your troupe," I said.

"Good thoughts, I hope," said Bets.

"Your performance at the Dunsworth's. . . . It was like a fairy tale," I said.

Isabelle laughed. The sound twinkled in the air.

"Like a fairy tale come true," I added. "The dancing, and the poetry, and the lanterns in the trees, and your costumes. You looked like Greek gods and goddesses."

"I do fancy myself a god in my better moments," said Raymond, running a hand through his hair.

Bets cuffed him on the ear. "Don't go getting a big head," she said.

"Ha!" he said. "Not likely, with you around."

"Lord, what fools these mortals be," said Isabelle.

"That's from *Midsummer Night's Dream!*" I said.

She nodded. "Act Three, Scene Two."

"I love Shakespeare," I said. "And my neighbor, Mr. Prenderwinkel, is going to be in *The Tempest*. At the California Theatre. He thinks I could be an actress someday."

"*The* Mr. Prenderwinkel?" said Artie. "The Shakespearean actor?"

"Yup," I said.

"How marvelous!" said Isabelle.

"Impressive," said Raymond.

"Prenderwinkel would know," said Artie. "If he said you could be an actress—"

"*Of course* she can be an actress," said Isabelle.

I beamed. "You think so, too?"

"Why not?"

"I don't know," I said. "I wasn't sure . . ." I sighed. "Perhaps I'll be an actress someday, but I'm not going to be an actress any time soon. My Aunt Phyllis is awfully old-fashioned."

"What difference does it make what your aunt thinks?" said Isabelle.

"Because I'm staying with my aunt and uncle while my mother and father are away, and my aunt won't let me see Mr. Prenderwinkel perform, and our class is going to perform scenes from *Romeo and Juliet*, and she won't let me be in it, and she's never even been to the theater but she thinks the theater is thoroughly unrespectable and that acting is scandalous and actors are not to be trusted."

They all laughed. I felt my cheeks coloring up.

"I didn't mean you!" I said.

"But your Aunt Phyllis does," said Isabelle. "We're exactly what she means. Especially Raymond. Right, Ray?"

Raymond roared with laughter.

"It's not so funny," I said. "You don't have to live with Aunt Phyllis."

"You are feeling the inexorable pull of the stage," said Isabelle. "You will never be able to resist, and therefore you must surrender to the Spirit of the Theater. Besides, if your Aunt Phyllis saw you act I'm sure she'd change her mind."

"Do you think so?"

"Aunt Phyllis sounds like a difficult woman," said Isabelle.

"Very difficult," I said, nodding.

"Raymond, stop laughing!" said Bets, pulling on his arm. "Please forgive our brother, Penelope. Sometimes his head is filled with cotton balls."

"*The lunatic, the lover, and the poet are of imagination all compact,*" said Isabelle. "That means you, Ray. At least the lunatic and the poet part."

At that they all roared again. I marveled at their easy manner.

It must be wonderful to have brothers and a sister to laugh with, I thought.

"C'mon, we have to practice," said Bets.

Isabelle took my hand. "You come, too."

"Where?" I said.

"To the clearing beyond the trees," she said. *"I know a bank where the wild thyme blows, Where oxlips and nodding violet grows—"* "That's *Midsummer Night's Dream* again!" I said.

"Right you are," said Artie.

Isabelle led me to a small glade surrounded by eucalyptus trees and told me to sit. I folded my legs beneath me. The trees smelled spicy.

"Artie, you stand there," said Isabelle. "Bets, like this. Ray, you're in front, facing the audience."

Isabelle arranged Artie and Bets on one side of the glade, their arms around each other. Then she crossed the glade and turned to face me. Rising onto her toes, she stretched out her arms.

"When do I start?" said Raymond.

"I'll let you know," she said.

She skipped toward Artie and Bets and circled them three times, her gown fluttering in the breeze. Stopping in front of them in a kind of half curtsy, she twisted her body from side to side, waving her hands in the air as if playing an invisible harp.

"Now, Ray," she whispered.

Raymond began to recite. *"She walks in beauty, like the night."*

Isabelle took a deep breath. It seemed to fill not just her lungs but her whole body. She rose once more onto her toes and began to walk very slowly across the glade, holding her head like a queen, so light on her feet that she seemed to barely touch the ground. I felt lifted up, as if she were raising me to a place where time had stopped.

"And all that's best of dark and bright, Meet in her aspect and her eyes," said Raymond.

Isabelle floated across the glade. As the poem continued, she reached toward the ground as if embracing the earth. She twirled, throwing back her head and lifting her arms toward the sky. As the twirling slowed she said, "Artie and Bets, skip over to me and bow."

"Not again!" said Bets.

"She fancies herself a queen," said Artie.

"Not a queen, a goddess!" cried Isabelle.

Bets made a face and took Artie's hand. They skipped to Isabelle and kneeled.

Isabelle dropped her arms. "And that's where the Beethoven comes in," she said.

Artie nodded. "It'll work." He plopped down on the dirt.

"Penelope, what'd you think?" asked Isabelle.

It took me a minute to find my voice, and when I finally found it, I didn't know what to say. "It was . . . it was . . . more than beautiful," I said.

"Thanks to Lord Byron," said Raymond.

"Who?" I said.

"The poet."

"And the dancing, of course," said Isabelle. "But did you think the dancing went with the poem?"

"Oh, yes!" I said.

She walked over to me. When she was dancing she had seemed taller, but now that it was over, she had resumed her normal size. I wondered what kind of magic could do that.

Artie pulled a watch out of his pocket. "Almost four," he said.

I jumped up. "I have to go," I said. "Aunt Phyllis will be furious if she finds out I went off alone."

"What will she do?" asked Bets.

Raymond grinned. "Boil her alive."

Bets glared at him. "Stop it!"

"Will you be rehearsing in the park again?" I asked.

Isabelle shrugged.

"Maybe," said Raymond.

"Depends," said Artie.

"On what?" I said.

Bets shook her head. "What they mean is that we're terribly

disorganized and we never know what will happen tomorrow."

"It's almost November," said Artie.

Raymond nodded. "Getting cold."

"And the rainy season is coming," said Isabelle. "Why don't you come visit us at home sometime? When you need to get away from your Aunt Phyllis. And don't listen to her opinions about the theater. You should audition for your class play. She'll never know."

In my mind's eye I saw Aunt Phyllis's frowning face.

"I'll think about it," I said. "Thank you for letting me watch."

I hurried away. When I reached the edge of the grove, I turned to wave. Isabelle was already practicing a new step, and the others were huddled together, deep in conversation.

I tried to find Aldy, but he was nowhere to be seen. It didn't matter. I floated back to Aunt Phyllis and Uncle Henry, my head in the air. As I neared Aunt Phyllis, however, my footsteps became heavy. How could I surrender to the Spirit of the Theater if she wouldn't let me be in the play?

CHAPTER NINETEEN

"The Play's the Thing"

Consuela ran to me in the school yard, her skirts flying. "Do you . . . want to practice . . . a scene together for the . . . audition?" she asked, all out of breath.

"I can't," I said.

"You can't? Why not?"

"I'm not supposed to," I said, kicking into the ground. "Aunt Phyllis says I'm not allowed."

"But we've been waiting forever."

"I know," I said. "And now I'm in a terrible predict-ament."

"What about your uncle? Did you ask him?"

"No. He put Aunt Phyllis in charge of me."

"What about your parents? Perhaps you could write to your parents."

"It takes *months* for letters to get to Hawaii and back," I said.

I was silent for a minute while I thought about what to do. Consuela was silent, too.

Finally I said, "My mother would let me. I know she would. She approves of Shakespeare. Not like Aunt Phyllis."

I looked at Consuela. I bit my lip. I made up my mind. "I'm going to audition anyway," I said. "No one will know."

Her mouth made a little "o" of surprise.

"I'm sure Mama wouldn't mind," I said. "She knows how I feel about the stage."

"But isn't that lying?" she said.

"No," I said. "It's . . . it's . . . make believe. It's acting."

"Are you sure?"

"Of course I'm sure!" I said.

I looked around the yard. I didn't want anyone to hear.

"Wait," I said. "Come over here."

I pulled Consuela to the side of the yard, next to the wooden fence. Drawing her close, I said, "You mustn't tell a soul that Aunt Phyllis doesn't want me to perform."

"But what about Aldy? Doesn't he know? And what about Violet? And Petunia? They'll tattle on you."

"Aldy doesn't care. He won't tell. Petunia won't find out, she's only in fourth grade. And Violet, well . . . Miss High-and-Mighty thinks she's too important to pay attention to what sixth graders do."

"But what about Miss Adelaide? What will you do when she asks for the permission slip?"

"Oh," I said. I hated to conceal the truth from Miss Adelaide. I picked at a splinter on the fence. "Miss Adelaide wants me to be in the play. It was our idea. We thought of it. In our imaginations. She always says to use our imaginations."

"What if your aunt finds out?"

"Well, she won't. She can't. She disapproves of the theater so much she won't even come. But if for some reason she did come, she'd be so impressed—with my acting—that . . . that . . ."

"That she'd forgive you!"

"That's right! She'd forgive me! That's just what I was thinking!" I looked around to make sure no one had heard. "Shhh!" I said, putting a finger to my mouth.

"She'd be very angry," she whispered.

"I know," I whispered back. "But my mother . . ."

I pictured Aunt Phyllis's angry face. I imagined her telling Mama that I was a headstrong and disobedient child.

I hit the fence with my hand. "Consuela, I have to," I said. "I have to be in it. How could I watch someone else be Juliet? It's *Shakespeare!*"

"But how will you get to school on the night of the performance without anyone finding out?"

I hadn't thought of that.

"I'll have to sneak out. That's all. Aldy'll be my lookout."

"And the permission slip?"

"I'll sign it myself."

She gasped. I looked away.

"I think we should do the balcony scene for the audition," I said.

"I suppose," she said. "Are you sure?"

I nodded. The first bell rang.

"Let's go," I said. "I don't want to be late."

For the next two weeks, Consuela and I practiced every day after school. We recited our lines and worked on our gestures. When Aunt Phyllis asked me why I was home so late, I didn't have to lie. I said I was working on a special project for Miss Adelaide.

On the day of the audition, I couldn't concentrate on schoolwork. The whole classroom was buzzing. Miss Adelaide kept telling us to calm down. I scribbled a note and passed it to Consuela.

"Do you think she'll pick me for Juliet?"

She passed a note back. "You're a good actress."

I wrote another note. "Do you think Linden will be Romeo?"

She giggled and nodded.

"Girls," said Miss Adelaide. "If I see any more notes, both of you will be sitting in the corner."

After school, Miss Adelaide made us all wait in the hall while we took turns auditioning. When our turn came, I said to Consuela, "Break a leg."

"You, too," she said.

Then we performed our scene for Miss Adelaide. I was Juliet, and Consuela was Romeo. We were brilliant.

Afterwards, in the hall, Consuela and I put our heads together.

"I thought we did well, didn't you?" I said.

"Except for that one line where I made a mistake," said Consuela.

"It was a very small mistake," I said, patting her on the arm. "Do you think Miss Adelaide liked our audition?"

"I hope so," she said.

"Me, too," I said. "With all my heart."

The next day, before the bell rang, everyone was talking at once. It seemed as if in the whole wide world there were only two questions: Who would play Juliet? Who would play Romeo? We didn't have to wait too long to find out, as Miss Adelaide made the announcement first thing.

"Children," she said. "May I have your attention, please? I would like to announce the results of the audition."

I held my breath.

"Class, for our performance in December we will recite sonnets and perform the prologue and two scenes from *Romeo and Juliet*." She bent over her notebook. "Now let's see. Myrtle, you may recite sonnet number eighteen. Diana, you did a lovely job with sonnet number twenty-nine. Albert, for you, sonnet number . . ."

I wiggled in my seat. My foot started to tap.

"Now, for the scenes from *Romeo and Juliet*," said Miss Adelaide. "The balcony scene, and the slaying of Benvolio and Tybalt."

I clutched the sides of my desk. I heard the magic words.

"In the balcony scene, Penny will play Juliet, and Consuela will be the understudy."

I nearly swooned.

"Linden, you will play Romeo."

Someone snickered. I think it was Horace. Miss Adelaide frowned.

"Chester is to recite the Prologue. Jacob, you will play Mercutio. Edwin will be Benvolio. Since not many boys auditioned, we will need one more boy to come forward and volunteer for the role of Tybalt."

Horace snickered again.

"Thank you, Horace, you may be Tybalt. Now, I want to say a few more words about the poetry portion of the program. . . ."

I didn't hear the rest. My head was spinning.

Miss Adelaide sees I'm talented.

Mama and Papa would be so proud of me.

Someday I'll be a famous actress and I'll look back and see that this was the beginning.

I raised my hand.

"Miss Adelaide, why can't we do the whole play?"

Miss Adelaide smiled. "Penny, I'm sure you'll be able to exercise your dramatic powers in a few scenes. Memorizing that much Shakespearean language will be challenge enough."

"I already memorized some of my part," I said.

Horace groaned.

"Nevertheless," said Miss Adelaide. "I think staging the entire play would be too large an undertaking. Now let's continue with our reading assignment."

But I couldn't concentrate on reading. All I could think about was the play.

That afternoon I walked home with Aldy. Aldy walked, that is. I skipped.

"Aldy?" I said.

"What?"

"You mustn't tell your mother or father or sisters that I'm in the play. It's a secret. Do you promise?"

"If Mother finds out—"

"What will she do?"

"Punishments," he said. "Bad punishments."

I didn't want to think about Aunt Phyllis and her punishments. "She won't find out," I said.

"What should I tell her when she asks why you're late coming home?"

"Tell her I'm staying after school to work on a special project for Miss Adelaide."

"How will you get to the evening performance?"

"I'll sneak out. You'll make sure no one's looking."

He shook his head. "It'll never work."

"Aw, come on, Aldy," I said.

"All right," he grumbled.

We had reached the house. I followed him up the steps to the front door.

"Listen. Aldy. You've got to keep it a secret. Even though we're only doing two scenes, I don't think your mother—"

"I won't tell," he said, and he opened the door and went inside.

Oh, Lord, I thought. *Please don't let Aunt Phyllis find out about the play.*

CHAPTER TWENTY

The Kiss

We had been rehearsing for three weeks and we still hadn't done any acting.

The first week, Miss Adelaide said we had to learn stage directions. She said when you moved toward the audience you were moving "downstage," and when you moved away from the audience you were moving "upstage," and when you were sitting in the audience, "stage right" was on your left, but when you were standing on the stage facing the audience, "stage right" was on your right. The whole thing was so confusing it addled my brain.

"Your first challenge is to find your way around the stage," said Miss Adelaide.

My first challenge was to find my way around Aunt Phyllis, I thought.

The second week of rehearsal, Miss Adelaide said we had to learn how to walk onto a stage and "take command," and how to project our voices so that everyone could hear, and how to be aware at all times of where we were looking and how we were standing and what we were doing with our hands.

"When do we get to act?" I asked her.

"Soon," she said. "We are laying the groundwork."

So far my groundwork was fine. Aunt Phyllis didn't suspect a thing.

The third week of rehearsal, Miss Adelaide said it was time for us to memorize our lines. Thank goodness we were doing just two scenes. It would have taken us from now until the twentieth century to learn the whole play. Shakespeare wrote a long time ago, and his words were hard.

But the hardest thing about the play wasn't the words. It was the boys. As soon as they figured out that the balcony scene was a love scene, there was such a commotion that Miss Adelaide made them go outside to practice their sword fight. After that they began to tease Linden and me, especially at recess. Sometimes Linden would pop the teaser in the nose, but it didn't do much good. And they didn't even know about the kiss.

I must confess I was worried about the kiss. Of course, I knew that Miss Adelaide wouldn't make me kiss Linden. That would be unseemly. Still, there were certain lines that *hinted* at a kiss, and I dreaded having to say them in front of an audience. Especially an audience with boys in it.

Between the rules and the teasing and the thought of the kiss lines, I wondered if perhaps Aunt Phyllis had been right, and I shouldn't have been in the play. But I only wondered for a minute.

At the end of the third week of rehearsal Miss Adelaide announced that it was time to put some feeling into our lines, and that we would start doing so on the following Monday. As we were leaving the school yard, I pulled Consuela aside.

"I'm worried about the balcony scene," I said.

"Why?" she said. "Miss Adelaide said it's coming along quite nicely. Linden finally memorized his lines, and your lines always sound good. Just remember to say every word clearly. E-nun-ci-ate."

I shook my head. "That's not what I mean." I leaned in closer and lowered my voice. "It's the kiss," I said.

She looked surprised. "What kiss?"

"The part where Juliet says, *'What satisfaction canst thou have tonight?'* and Romeo says, *'The exchange of thy love's faithful vow for mine,'* and then later Juliet says, *'My bounty is as boundless as the sea, my love as deep; the more I give to thee The more I have, for both are infinite.'"*

"That means they kiss?" she asked.

"I think so."

"I didn't know they kiss. Does it say they kiss?"

"No. I just feel it."

"What do you mean?"

My face was getting hot. "I mean, um, if Juliet's love is as deep as the sea, wouldn't she kiss Romeo?"

She didn't look convinced.

"It's a love scene," I said. "Actors always kiss in a love scene."

"But we're not real actors. We're kids."

"It doesn't matter. Everyone will know they're *supposed* to kiss. Especially when we put *feelings* in our lines. Which we're supposed to do on Monday. And if we say our lines with feelings during the performance, the audience will know about the kiss. And they won't like it. They'll think it isn't proper. And what if Aunt Phyllis finds out?"

Consuela's big, black eyes got even bigger.

"Don't you think it will be awkward?" I said. "Saying those lines with everyone watching?"

"I didn't know they kissed." She began to blush. "What if you're sick, and I have to be Juliet? Does Miss Adelaide know about the kiss? Will she make you say those lines?"

"They're part of the scene."

"And will Linden agree to it?"

"He auditioned," I said.

"He didn't know there were kiss parts!"

I shrugged.

"Oh dear," she said. "What should we do?"

"Well, I'm not going to ask Linden what he thinks," I said. "We had better ask Miss Adelaide."

"Okay," she said. "You ask. I'll come."

"All right," I said.

We approached Miss Adelaide on Monday before school.

"Miss Adelaide, may we have a minute, please?" I said.

"Certainly, Penny. Good morning, Consuela. What's on your minds?"

"In private," I said.

We went into the hall.

"Miss Adelaide," I began. "It's . . ."

She looked at me sympathetically.

". . . the balcony scene," said Consuela.

"Yes, the balcony scene," I said.

"Oh," said Miss Adelaide. "Don't worry, girls, it's coming along quite nicely."

"Um, that's not what we mean," I said.

"You're both doing an excellent job," she said. "Your parents will be proud of you."

"My parents are away," I said in a small voice.

"Oh, yes, of course," said Miss Adelaide. "I forgot. Well, then, Penny, Consuela's parents will be proud of her, and your aunt and uncle will be proud of you."

I smiled weakly. I cleared my throat. I wanted to ask about the kiss, but the words stuck. I looked at Consuela.

Consuela, say something, I thought.

"And now, if you'll excuse me, girls," said Miss Adelaide, "I must get the day started. We have plenty to do. Please come into the classroom."

We followed Miss Adelaide back into the room.

"What about the kiss parts?" whispered Consuela.

"I didn't know what to say," I whispered back.

"Girls, take your seats, please. Good morning, class," said Miss Adelaide.

I scowled. *I'll never be an actress*, I thought, *if I can't say what I truly feel.*

All that day I worried about the kiss. By the time school ended, my tummy was churning.

"All right, children, everyone may go except for Linden, Consuela, and Penny. Boys, practice your swordplay in the hall."

There was a rustle of books and coats as everyone got up to leave. When the last voice had faded down the hallway, Miss Adelaide turned to the three of us.

"Now then," she said. "Today we will work on saying our lines with some dramatic flair. Then we'll put the whole balcony scene together. Linden, would you please help me carry our 'balcony' out of the coatroom?"

Linden jumped up to help Miss Adelaide fetch the wooden platform that was our balcony.

As they pushed it into place she said, "Thank you, Linden. All right, now let's put the finishing touches on this scene."

I had a moment of panic. "Finishing touches" could mean only one thing. Saying the kiss lines with feelings.

"Um, do we have to?" I said.

"Excuse me?" said Miss Adelaide.

"Do we have to put the finishing touches on the scene?"

"Of course. The scene still needs some work, and we don't have that many days left, what with Thanksgiving next week."

She must have seen the look on my face, for then she said, "Penny, what's the matter? Weren't you counting the days until the performance? Are you getting cold feet?"

"No, um, it's nothing," I said.

"All right," said Miss Adelaide. "Consuela? Would you like to go first? We should make sure you have a good feeling for the role of Juliet, since you're the understudy."

I held my breath, hoping that Consuela would agree. I knew I shouldn't wish such a thing, but I couldn't help it. I truly, truly, didn't want to say those kiss lines.

"I'd be happy to, Miss Adelaide," said Consuela.

I exhaled.

Then Consuela added, "But I think it's Penny's turn today."

Oh no! My heart started to pound.

"All right," said Miss Adelaide, moving some chairs out of the way. "Girls, let's practice your entrances first. Remember, step onto the platform gracefully as you say your first line."

She demonstrated. She was very graceful.

We practiced stepping onto the platform for a few minutes. Linden watched. I was so nervous it was hard to be graceful, but Miss Adelaide didn't seem to notice. Finally she told Consuela to sit.

Linden brushed a lock of hair off his forehead. I wanted to disappear. For a moment it was very quiet in the room. Some tiny bits of dust swirled around in a ray of sunlight.

"He jests at scars that never felt a wound," said Linden.

"Wait a moment, please," said Miss Adelaide. "I believe we'll start in the middle today. For a change of pace. You're both on the platform. Side by side. Like this." She put us next to each other, facing the audience, our shoulders almost touching.

"Good. Now, Penny, why don't you begin at '*How cam'st thou hither, tell me, and wherefore?*'"

I took a little step sideways. I couldn't bear to stand so close if we were going to put in feelings. It would be too, too embarrassing.

"Penny?"

"How cam'st thou hither, tell me, and wherefore?" I mumbled. *"The orchard walls are high and hard to climb; And the place death, considering who thou art, if any of my kinsmen find thee here."*

"Louder, Penny."

"With love's light wings did I o'erperch these walls," said Linden.

My eye twitched. We said a few more lines. When we got to the part where I have a long speech, Miss Adelaide interrupted.

"Penny," she said, "why don't you look at Linden when you say *'O gentle Romeo,'* and continue to look at him until the end of your speech."

I glanced at Linden. "Shouldn't I be looking at the audience? Or at a spot on the wall at the back of the audience, as we did last week?"

"We'll try this today. To get a feeling for the lines."

I wanted to get a feeling. Truly I did. But it was hard to look at Linden.

I continued with my speech. His eyes shifted left, then right. He fiddled with a button on his shirt.

"Louder, dear," said Miss Adelaide.

I was already loud. How could I be any louder? *"My true love's passion,"* I said, clutching my chest for emphasis.

"Hands still, please."

I reached the end of my speech.

"Go ahead, Linden," said Miss Adelaide.

"Do I have to look at her?" he asked.

I wanted to sink right down into my shoes.

"Yes, dear."

Linden scratched his head. "All right."

He recited some lines.

Perhaps he doesn't care for me, I thought.

He leaned toward me. *"Oh, wilt thou leave me so unsatisfied?"* he said, his eyes widening.

He was grinning. I bit my lip. Was he making fun of me?

"My bounty is . . ." I said. *"My bounty is . . ."* I couldn't remember the line.

"As boundless as the sea," said Miss Adelaide.

I wanted to run right out of the room. I was trying to put feelings into the lines, but all I felt was confused.

"Sorry," I said.

I couldn't wait for the scene to be over. As we neared the end, I felt a burst of energy. *"Good-night, good-night!"* I said, cheerfully.

"That's it, Penny," said Miss Adelaide. "Nice and loud. Now let's hear those last lines clearly. Enunciate."

Was this what it felt like to put in feelings? I didn't think so. *"Parting. Is. Such. Sweet. Sorrow,"* I said, e-nun-ci-a-ting every word.

"Sleep dwell upon thy eyes," said Linden, staring at me as he finished the scene.

I looked away. What was he feeling?

Acting is so hard, I thought. My face felt hot. I wanted to cry.

"That was a beginning," said Miss Adelaide. "I think the more we rehearse, the more comfortable you will feel with the lines. Let's try it again, with Consuela as Juliet."

I sat down, wishing I was far away. In England, perhaps. Or Italy. Somewhere across a wide ocean.

CHAPTER TWENTY-ONE

In the Garden

As the days went by, saying my lines didn't get any easier. I wanted to put in feelings, but I didn't know how. I was in torment.

One afternoon I found myself practicing in the backyard, whispering my lines so that no one would hear. The rain-soaked garden twinkled in the sun as I strutted across the grass. As I neared the hedge, I spied Mr. Prenderwinkel bending over the rose bushes next door.

"Mr. Prenderwinkel!" I called.

He stood up and looked around.

"It's me! Penelope."

"Ah, Penelope. How came you so called?" he said.

"It was my father's idea," I said, slipping through the wet hedge. "It comes from the ancient Greeks. He likes the ancient Greeks. Especially Homer."

"Ah, yes, the wine-dark sea," he said.

"What?" I said.

"Nothing, my dear. How goes it with you, Penelope?"

"Miss Adelaide, my teacher, is letting us recite scenes from *Romeo and Juliet*."

"Splendid!" he said. "Then we are both Children of the Bard."

"Children of who?"

"Shakespeare," he said. "The Bard of Avon. The Dean of Dramaturge. The Visionary of Versification. The Progenitor of Poesy."

"Oh," I said.

"And you are?"

"Penelope," I said.

He laughed. "No, no. In the play. Your role."

"Oh," I said. "Oh." I could feel my cheeks coloring up. "I'm Juliet."

"Verily?" he said. "Why then, a brilliant Juliet you must be."

"I don't know," I said. "I don't feel brilliant. I feel confused. I don't know what to do with my hands. I don't know where to look. I feel so awkward. Miss Adelaide says everything will fall into place, and right now we're just practicing. I mean rehearsing. But I wish I could have elocution lessons so I could learn the proper gestures. Like a real actress. And I want to know how to pronounce the words so I don't sound silly, and how do you recite a quiet scene and say your lines so a person in the last row can hear you?"

"Sounds like you're ripe for elocution lessons," said Mr. Prenderwinkel.

"That's just what I thought! Mama said she'd let me take lessons when she and Papa get home, but only if I've been a good girl while they're away. So I have to be a good girl, whether I like it or not. And I don't always like it."

He nodded. He wasn't just being neighborly—he truly understood. I smiled at him. He bent down and started pulling up some weeds. I thought perhaps I should tell him that I wasn't being such a good girl, that Aunt Phyllis didn't know I was in the play. But I was afraid he might think less of me, so I held my tongue. A bumblebee buzzed over the roses.

Mr. Prenderwinkel stood up, took a pair of scissors out of his pocket, and began to snip off some orange roses. Water drops fell from the ruffled petals.

"Smell," he said, holding out the roses.

I smelled. They were sweet and spicy.

"Feel," he said.

I felt. The petals were soft as silk.

"Mr. Prenderwinkel?"

"Yes?"

"How do you not get distracted?"

"Distracted? Are you distracted, my dear? You seem to exhibit prodigious powers of concentration."

"Sometimes during my scenes with Linden I get distracted. He says his Romeo lines, and I forget what I'm supposed to say next. Then Miss Adelaide has to come to my rescue and tell me the line. It's so embarrassing."

Mr. Prenderwinkel raised one eyebrow. "Does Linden look at you when he speaks his lines?"

"Oh, it isn't Linden's fault. It isn't anything he does. It's me. I think there's something wrong with me."

"Tell me more about this Linden."

"He's . . ." I had to stop and think for a moment. "He's . . ."

"Handsome?" said Mr. Prenderwinkel, snipping another rose.

"Quite handsome."

"A perfect Romeo?"

"Yes."

"Then you will be a perfect Juliet."

"How? How can I be a perfect Juliet?"

"The way you feel about Linden is exactly the way Juliet felt about Romeo. You must reveal that to the audience."

"Oh," I said slowly. "But . . . but . . . I don't want anyone in class to know how I feel about Linden. They'd make fun of me."

He smiled. "No one need know you feel that way about Linden. They'll simply see a Juliet who loves her Romeo."

"Oh," I said. "I thought acting was more about learning the proper gestures." I planted my feet wide apart and held one hand against my brow. "Like this. See? Don't I look . . . um . . . stricken with grief?"

He stopped clipping his roses and looked at me. "In my opinion," he said, "actors who insist on mannerisms and pompous declamation are an insult to the art of the theater. Such carryings-on might be sufficient for your pantomimes and your extravaganzas, but if you want to be a great tragedienne—and I sense, Penelope, that you do—your art must convey *true feeling*. That which comes from the depths of the human heart. No, my dear, you must forsake such contrivances as empty gesture. Then, and only then, will you take your first steps toward becoming a true actress." He smiled. "And I sense, with all my being, that you are doing so at this very moment. Why, in the blink of an eye you'll be the genuine article."

"Genuine article?"

"An actress."

"Oh! Do you truly think so?"

"Absolutely. I can see it in you already."

I beamed at him and began to twirl in delight. He laughed. "So you intend to become a dancer, as well?"

"I don't care if it's acting or dancing or turning tumblesaults, as long as I get to do it in front of an audience!"

"It's just too bad about your aunt," he said. "I pity her."

I stopped twirling. "Pity her? Why?"

"Think of what she's missing."

"Do you mean it's sad that she's never been to the theater?"

"She's never had her heart touched, her passions aroused, her sympathies stirred. What moves the spirit, Penelope? Everyday life? Your aunt is afraid of the theater. And of actors."

"Afraid?" I couldn't imagine Aunt Phyllis being afraid of anything.

"Why do you think your aunt disapproves of the theater?"

"Because it's not proper."

"It's more than that. The theater is larger than life, much larger. And actors seem larger than life to her, too. Our actions. Our feelings. That scares her. To some people, emotions that strong are frightening. Emotions that strong are wild and untamable."

I thought of the picture of the young Aunt Phyllis in the dining room, the one with the lively eyes. She hadn't always been so stiff. I remembered the look on her face at the musicale, when Penelope was playing the violin. She had feelings, I knew she did. They were just invisible. I listened intently.

"The theater connects people to each other, Penelope, and those who give themselves to the theater must give themselves heart and soul."

"I would give myself heart and soul," I said.

"Of course you would. But it isn't easy. An actor has to dig very deep to find emotions that will sway an audience. An actor must bare his soul. It takes effort and discipline. An actor must be both disciplined and wild."

"Cornelius! Supper!" Mrs. Prenderwinkel called out the window. "Curtain in three hours!"

"My beloved calls," said Mr. Prenderwinkel. He handed me a rose. "I'm delighted to hear of your good fortune in landing the lead, my dear. It sounds like you're making excellent progress toward your chosen profession. Remember—if you allow your own feelings to shine through the character, you can't go wrong. And now I must take my leave, fair Penelope. *Parting is such sweet sorrow.*"

I blushed again. "Thank you, Mr. Prenderwinkel."

He bowed. "A pleasure, my dear."

Later, as I pressed the rose between the pages of my Shakespeare book, I marveled at the wonderful gift I had been given, to be able to talk with a real actor. I thought about what Mr. Prenderwinkel had said, and I even began to feel a bit sorry for Aunt Phyllis. How dull her life must be without the theater. If only she could see the truth.

But what did Mr. Prenderwinkel mean when he said an actor had to be disciplined and wild at the same time? And how could I follow his advice? Did I have the courage to bare my soul?

CHAPTER TWENTY-TWO

Caught

I tried to follow Mr. Prenderwinkel's advice about showing my feelings in my scene with Linden. It was hard at first, because I thought Linden would laugh at me. But he didn't, and as the day of the performance approached, I became more and more excited.

Then, on the Tuesday after Thanksgiving, everyone began to make mistakes at rehearsal. Even me! It was as if all the work of the past few weeks had started to come undone.

"Boys and girls, please calm down," said Miss Adelaide. "I can see that you're getting nervous. You've been working very hard, and I expect everything to go beautifully on Thursday. Remember—hard work is the foundation of success."

As always, Miss Adelaide's words were comforting. But Horace's behavior was not. Because the performance was in two days, we had to practice it from beginning to end, which meant everybody got to watch the balcony scene. When the kiss part came, I hesitated.

"Go ahead, please," said Miss Adelaide. "Project your voice, Penny. Remember to *boom*."

I said the line, but I didn't *boom*. Horace hooted anyway.

Miss Adelaide held up her hand. "Just a moment please," she said. "Horace, that is quite enough. I trust you will be better behaved on Thursday, when your parents are present. Romeo, continue."

As Linden went on, I could feel myself blush. He spoke with a lot of feeling, more than I'd seen in him before. When we got to the second kiss line, his voice cracked a little, and I could hear Horace snort. Linden's eyes flickered away from mine, and he said the next line as if he were talking to someone behind me. I turned my head to see if there was anyone there, but there wasn't. I wondered if he would do that during the performance.

Somehow we managed to finish the scene without further interruption. Miss Adelaide seemed pleased.

"Get a good night's sleep, everyone," she said. "Tomorrow is our last rehearsal."

Wednesday dawned chilly and gray. My nerves were so agitated that I couldn't eat breakfast. Outside, it was drizzling, and by the time I arrived at school, my hair was a curly mess.

After school Miss Tumleigh came to watch. She sat through the whole rehearsal and clapped hard at the end. She murmured a few words of encouragement and left. We gathered around Miss Adelaide.

"That was splendid, children," she said. "Tomorrow you'll be wonderful. Boys, remember, white shirt and tie, please, and dark trousers. Girls, white blouse and skirt. Now go home."

On the way out the door, Consuela told me I was brilliant.

"Do you truly think so?" I said.

"Of course," she said. "Are you nervous? I am. Terribly. And I'm only the understudy."

"You're a very good understudy," I said, patting her arm.

"Thanks," she said. "But are you nervous?"

"I was before, but now I'm better. Miss Tumleigh seemed to like it, don't you think? Did I deliver my lines with flair?"

She nodded.

"If only Mama and Papa could come," I said. "Or Mr. Prenderwinkel. Or Isabelle."

"Isabelle?"

"You know. Isabelle Grey. The girl I told you about, the one who has an acting troupe with her brothers and sister. Remember? *Dancer and actress extraordinaire?*"

"Oh, yes," she said solemnly. "*Dancer and actress extraordinaire.*" We giggled.

"Penny?"

"Mmm?"

"You did say your lines with a great deal of flair."

I burst into a smile. "I did? Thank you! But I'm still quite anxious."

"Why?"

"I can't help worrying about Aunt Phyllis. What if Violet finds out? What if she tells Aunt Phyllis? You know what kind of person Violet is."

"If Violet knew about the play she would have told by now," she said.

"Yes, I suppose so. I suppose it's silly of me to worry. All right, I won't. See you tomorrow."

"Bye," she said, and started to walk away.

I grabbed her arm. "Consuela? Do you know what?"

"What?"

"You are my best, best friend."

"You're my best friend, too," she said, and smiled.

Outside, the sky had cleared. I hurried home and went straight to my room. I wanted to look over *Romeo and Juliet* one more time. I curled up on the bed with Miranda, opened my Shakespeare, and began to read. Toward the end of Act III, I heard a ruckus in the hallway. I got up and poked my head out the door just as Aldy came storming past, with Violet close behind.

"I'm going to tell," she yelled.

He whirled around. "Don't you dare!" he said.

"You can't stop me!"

"I can too. I'll . . . I'll . . ."

"You'll what?" Her lips curled into a sneer. "Since when does Mother allow anyone to be in a play at school?"

He glared at her. "Since now," he said, stomping down the hallway and slamming his door.

Violet started to follow him down the hall, but thought better of it. Instead she turned and fixed me with an icy stare.

"Tell me more about this play," she said.

CHAPTER TWENTY-THREE

The Worst Thing That Could Happen

"What play?" I said, backing away from her.

She took a step toward me. "You're in the class play, aren't you?" she said. "I was delivering a note to Mr. Ducree from my teacher, and I just happened to see the announcement on the bulletin board in the sixth grade hallway. With the *cast list*. You lied to Mother! You ungrateful—"

"I am not a liar," I said, pulling myself up to my full height. "I am an actress."

"Yes," she said, "and you've done some excellent acting, haven't you?" She took another step toward me. "You've certainly fooled Mother. You've pulled the wool over her eyes completely. You're not an actress. You're nothing but a liar. And after all she's done for you! Sending you to comportment classes and everything. She should've known better than to waste her money on you. Imagine someone like *you* learning manners. You can't even match your dress and your hair ribbon."

Violet edged closer. "We didn't have to take you in for six months, you know. Did you think we wanted you here?"

"Yes, do you think we wanted you here?" said Petunia, who had appeared out of nowhere.

Violet cocked her head to one side. A new look came over

145

her face. She leaned in so close, I could smell the rosemary oil in her hair.

"I don't have to tell Mother," she hissed. "We could make a trade."

"What kind of trade?"

"How about that paisley shawl of yours?"

"That's my mother's shawl." I wanted to punch her.

"I'll pay you for it. I bet you could use some money. Your father doesn't make very much, that's what Mother says. You could go see that Mr. Prenderwinkel in his play. Or buy yourself a new pair of shoes."

She laughed. Petunia laughed, too.

"You can't bribe me," I said. "You don't deserve a stitch of that shawl. You don't even deserve to look at it."

"Fine!" she spat. "We'll see what you think when I tell Mother you're in the play."

At that very moment I heard the front door open.

"Yoo-hoo, I'm home," called Aunt Phyllis, back from her meeting. "Early supper tonight, children. Please be prompt. Your father has an engagement."

"Mother!" Violet called, and ran for the stairs.

I couldn't move. My mind was racing. What could I do? My secret was about to be revealed. My life, ruined. My extraordinary future, crushed.

Petunia was watching me. I pushed her aside, ran to my room, and shut the door.

I'll run away, I thought, tearing open my wardrobe. *I'll run away and—*"

"Penelope Leuts Bailey, come down here this minute!" Aunt Phyllis called.

Oh, dear God, I thought.

"PE-NE-LO-PE!"

With shaking legs, I approached the stairs. Aunt Phyllis

stood at the bottom, her face twisted with anger. Behind her stood Violet, looking triumphant.

"Come with me," said Aunt Phyllis, grasping me by the arm. "Violet, I'll deal with you later."

"Me?" sputtered Violet. "What did I do?"

"Tattler!" snapped Aunt Phyllis, dragging me toward the study.

Violet tried to follow. "But Mother—" she protested.

"No buts!" yelled Aunt Phyllis, slamming the door in her face.

She whirled around. Her eyes were bulging. "You can't bamboozle me, young lady!" she said.

"Aunt Phyllis," I said.

"Silence!" she roared.

I hung my head.

"You wicked, wicked girl. You are no better than a common criminal," she said. "I don't even know how to begin to catalog your transgressions. Lying. Deceitfulness. Immodesty. And to think that you are a member of my own family. My own family! Where did you learn such tricks? Have you been speaking to that vaudevillian next door? Has he been up to some bedevilment or other? What kind of nefarious spell has he put you under?"

"He . . . Mr. Prenderwinkel. . . . It's not his fault! He—"

"I will not have any Lola Montez living under my roof! I simply won't have it!"

"The play—"

"I don't care a hang about your play! Not one whit! I expected mischief, I expected you to get into scrapes, but this! This goes beyond mischief. You have disgraced us all, Penelope, *disgraced* us with your prancing about in public and your silly notions about acting. Did you think you could be in this play and keep it from me? Did you think you could lie about it and not be caught? Do you think you can do anything that strikes your fancy in this world?"

"I didn't—"

"Don't be impertinent," she raged. She raised a hand as if to strike me, but stopped herself. "I shudder to contemplate what will become of a girl like you," she said, shaking her head. "What do you have to say for yourself?"

"I—"

"No! Stop! Never mind! What possible explanation could there be? Uncle Henry has it on good authority that your parents will be back soon. They will be informed, and they will have to deal with the long-term consequences of your outrageous behavior. For the moment, you are forbidden, *forbidden*, to be in this play. You are to go to your room without supper. Tomorrow I will speak to Miss Tumleigh. We will see if Uncle Henry has anything to add when he comes home. Which will be late tonight. You are excused."

She turned away from me, knocking into a large globe that stood on a table. The globe tipped and almost toppled. I reached out to steady it, but Aunt Phyllis stood in the way.

"Enough!" she said.

The globe crashed to the floor. Aunt Phyllis didn't even flinch. She walked to the door and flung it open. Violet and Petunia leapt back. They had been eavesdropping.

"Out of my way!" cried Aunt Phyllis, sweeping them aside.

I fled to my room and threw myself upon the bed. I buried my face in my pillow and wept bitter tears. Great sobs shook my chest. I thought they would never stop.

CHAPTER TWENTY-FOUR

The Escape

The room was dark when I awoke. I had fallen asleep with my clothes on. At first I thought it was the middle of the night. Then I noticed a faint sliver of light under the door.

After a while I heard the front door open. Uncle Henry was home. I clutched Miranda to my chest, fearful of what might happen next. What would Aunt Phyllis tell him? What would he do to me? Would he beat me with a wooden paddle?

I sat up. If she were going to talk to him in private, she'd do it in the study. The study was just below my bedroom. Perhaps I could hear.

I rose from the bed, knelt, and put my ear to the floor. I could hear voices, but I couldn't make out the words. They talked for a while. I heard a door close. Then there was silence.

I felt as if I couldn't breathe. I stumbled to the window and threw it open. The fresh air brought a measure of calm. A line from my psalm came into my head. I clasped my hands tight and whispered the words:

The Lord on high is mightier than the noise of many waters, yea, than the mighty waves of the sea.

I closed my eyes. In my mind I saw angry storm clouds and a

huge, dark wave. A fit of anger rose inside my chest.

How could Aunt Phyllis be so cruel?

I banged my head against the window frame.

I always knew what kind of person she was. And her stupid daughters, too! Didn't I tell Mama?

Downstairs, the grandfather clock struck twelve. I slammed the window shut and slunk back to bed.

Tomorrow Aunt Phyllis will drag me to school and tell Miss Tumleigh that I can't be in the play.

I grabbed my pillow and flung it to the floor.

Here I am, at the brink of my debut, and Aunt Phyllis is snatching it away. Why?

Because she's vile, that's why. All she cares about is being proper. She'll never understand about acting. Never!

It's all my fault. Why did I think I could fool Aunt Phyllis? Why did I think I could keep the play a secret?

No. Miss Adelaide believes in me. And Mr. Prenderwinkel said there was hope.

I picked up Miranda and shook her.

I must keep that hope alive, Miranda! I must!

The next morning Aunt Phyllis shook me awake. "Wash up, put on some fresh clothes, and meet me downstairs in ten minutes. And for goodness sake fix your hair."

I didn't answer.

"You won't be needing this any more," she said, snatching my Shakespeare book from the bedside table.

"Hey! That's mine!" I said.

"Hmph," she said, and, clutching the book to her chest, she left the room.

Mama's shawl had fallen on the floor. I picked it up and spread it on the bed. It was wrinkled, but the colors were as beautiful as ever. A tear dropped onto the wool. I wiped it off.

I washed and dressed as Aunt Phyllis had instructed, wrapped the shawl about me, and went downstairs. All the way to school, I walked behind Aunt Phyllis. When we got there, she went straight to the office and demanded to speak to Miss Tumleigh.

The clerk rose in haste, nearly knocking over her chair. "Yes, Mrs. Leuts, of course, Mrs. Leuts, please take a seat, she'll be with you in a moment."

Aunt Phyllis didn't take a seat. She just stood there with a tight grip on my hand.

In a minute Miss Tumleigh came out of her office. She was smiling, but her smile disappeared when she saw Aunt Phyllis's face.

"Good morning, Mrs. Leuts, what can I do for you today?" she said.

"Good morning," said Aunt Phyllis. "Penelope, wait here." She followed Miss Tumleigh into her office, and the door clicked shut behind them.

I sat while the clerk busied herself with paperwork. After a few minutes Miss Tumleigh came out, whispered something to the clerk, and went back in. The clerk got up and left. I could hear her heels clicking down the hall.

I looked at the clock. School was starting. What would happen when Miss Adelaide called the roll? She would say my name, and no one would answer. Aldy would break the news. Miss Adelaide would be upset. And Consuela would get to play Juliet.

I felt an ache in my chest. Then I smiled. It would make Consuela happy to play Juliet. She deserved to be happy.

The clerk did not return. Miss Adelaide came instead, with a worried look on her face. She put a hand on my arm.

"Are you all right?" she said.

I nodded. I couldn't speak, even to Miss Adelaide.

She went into Miss Tumleigh's office. Ten minutes went by.

At first I couldn't hear what they were saying, but soon their voices got louder.

Miss Adelaide: "But she gave me a signed permission slip!"

Aunt Phyllis: "I never signed anything."

Miss Adelaide: "I have it right here. Look."

There was silence. Then the talking started up again, but quietly. Finally, Aunt Phyllis came out.

"That's settled," she said.

I stared at the floor. I didn't want to know what was settled.

"Where are your manners? Stand up and look at me when I speak to you."

I stood and looked at her. But not at her eyes.

"You have been switched to Mr. Ducree. The play will go on without you—evidently there are parents in this city who approve of such things—but Miss Adelaide has been chastised for allowing your participation. You can report to Mr. Ducree as soon as Miss Tumleigh comes out. Come straight home after school. I will see you then."

She tried to sweep out of the room but nearly lost her balance as she reached for her skirts. She was wearing one of Mrs. Plumbottom's new dresses, without the bustle, and the change of shape caught her off guard.

"Hmph," she said, and left.

I slumped back into my seat. Presently, Miss Adelaide came out with Miss Tumleigh. I stood up. Miss Adelaide's eyes were red.

"Penny," she said.

I looked into her eyes and saw her disappointment.

"I hope . . ." she said.

What did she hope?

She didn't finish her sentence. She simply adjusted her glasses and left.

Miss Tumleigh had a grim look on her face. "You may proceed to Mr. Ducree's," she said.

"Yes, ma'am."

Miss Tumleigh turned to go back into her office. At the door she stopped. "And shame on you for lying to your aunt and forging her signature," she said.

The clerk stared at me. My face was burning. I walked out of the office and down the empty corridor. At the end of the hall I turned, but not toward Mr. Ducree's. I walked out the door and down the street. I didn't know where I was going. I only knew I wasn't going back. If I couldn't be in Miss Adelaide's class, then I wouldn't go to school at all. And I'd rather die in the street than go home to Aunt Phyllis.

I wiped my cheek. My face was wet. I didn't even know I'd been crying. I reached into my pocket for a handkerchief. Instead I found a crumpled white visiting card.

"Isabelle Grey. Taylor and Geary Streets. Dancer and Actress Extraordinaire."

I pressed the card to my chest.

I don't have to die in the street, I thought.

I can still be an actress.

I will take this card, and I will find Isabelle Grey.

CHAPTER TWENTY-FIVE

Searching for Isabelle

A storm was threatening as I set off in the direction of Mrs. Plumbottom's. I hurried down Washington Street and turned at Van Ness, crossing Clay, Sacramento, California, Pine, Bush. The wind was blowing hard. It began to rain. I drew Mama's shawl over my head and turned my shoulder to the wind.

I rounded the corner onto Sutter and raced through the commercial district. Where was Taylor and Geary? At Sutter and Taylor I turned again, but the next street was Polk. I tried a different direction—down one street, then another. No luck.

I had been running much of the way, but now, with a cramp in my side, I slowed to a walk and took shelter in the doorway of a hardware store. It was cold, and my forehead was damp with sweat. I huddled up against the building. An empty wagon rattled by, the driver hunched over the reins, his collar pulled up to his ears, his black slicker shiny and wet.

What if I can't find Isabelle?

What if I find her, but she won't take me in?

Through the store window I could see hammers and saws, nails and screws. There was a reflection in the window, too. It was a street sign.

It said:

T-E-E-R-T-S Y-R-A-E-G

The letters were backward on account of being a reflection. I puzzled them out.

S-T-R-E-E-T G-E-A-R—

I whipped around. How could I have been so close and not noticed?

I ran to the corner and checked the sign. Geary and Taylor. Taylor and Geary. Isabelle Grey, Dancer and Actress Extraordinaire, could not be far. But which house was hers?

"Isabelle! Isabelle Grey!"

My voice echoed off the buildings.

I knocked on the door of the house closest to me. No one answered. The door was unlocked, so I pushed it open. The building was old, its plaster walls cracked and peeling. There was a sign in the hallway with the names of the people who lived there.

Apartment #1 ETHELBERT KIPPERS
Apartment #2 MR. AND MRS. T.P. SKELLY
Apartment #3 R. BRAXTON FAMILY
Apartment #4 MRS. SHERMAN SNOWE
Apartment #5 GREY

Grey! I ran up three flights of stairs and knocked at apartment #5. The door swung open. I took a step forward and my knees nearly gave way.

"Isabelle," I gasped.

"Oh!" she said. "Hello. Come in!"

The front hall was crammed with furniture, the floor littered with shoes and bags. Piles of books and papers lay about, and in the corner a jumble of coats and hats overflowed from a coat rack onto the floor. I had never seen a room in such disarray.

"You're shivering," she said.

I couldn't speak. She sat me down and pulled off my wet

shoes and stockings, grabbed a blanket from a chest by the door, and flung it over me.

"Let's have some tea," she said, leading me to a small kitchen and laying my shoes and stockings by the stove.

She filled a teakettle at a sink piled high with dirty dishes. Then she set it on the stove and motioned for me to sit. My teeth were chattering.

"Sorry it's so cold," she said. "Mother's late with the rent and she couldn't pay the coal man, either. But we still have wood for the stove. Give me your shawl, I'll hang it up to dry."

My mind was frozen. "You . . . you have a mother?" I stammered. I had imagined that Isabelle and her brothers and sister lived by themselves, without parents.

"Of course. That's her, playing the piano in the parlor." She leaned toward me. "My mother is a woman on whom the muses smile," she said. "Mary Dora Grey, educated in music, dance, poetry, and the disappointments of love. Of course, I prefer to think I sprang fully grown from the brow of Zeus. But alas, I am mortal." She winked at me. "Now tell me, what mischief are you up to? Have you got yourself into a scrape?"

Before I could answer, the kettle began to boil. She pulled a chipped teacup out of the pile of dirty dishes, rinsed it out, and poured me a cup of tea with three lumps of sugar. Then she made room on the table by pushing a pile of newspapers onto the floor, and placed the cup in front of me. I drained it to the very bottom.

"Out with it now," she said. "Tell me why you've come."

"I . . ." I said, clearing my throat, "I thought . . ."

She didn't wait for me to finish, but took my hand and peered at my palm. "Look. Look at this line." She traced a finger down one of the lines on my hand. "You're a seeker. That's why you've come."

"I . . . I want to act," I said.

"Splendid!" she said. "Can you dance, too?"

I could feel the heat rising to my cheeks. "Not too well," I said. "Not like you. I never—"

"I knew it!" she said, slapping the table. "Penelope Leuts Bailey, you are an orphan child! A leaf blown by the wind! Have you run away? Tell me your story. From the beginning. And don't leave anything out."

"I'm . . . I'm not exactly an orphan," I said.

"I was speaking metaphorically," she said.

Whether it was the effect of the hot tea or Isabelle's kind face, I couldn't tell, but I felt warmer.

"It . . . it started back in June," I said, and proceeded to tell her everything that had happened to me since Mama sailed for Hawaii, right up to and including my hasty departure from school that morning. Isabelle sat motionless as the words poured forth.

"So you see why I've come," I concluded.

Isabelle whistled. "What a terrible woman. And that Violet!"

"I know."

"How could she object to the theater? The theater is noble. And Shakespeare! How could she dislike Shakespeare?"

She rose and began to stride back and forth, waving her arms in the air. "A Philistine is what she is, your Aunt Phyllis. Deaf to the call of the Inner Spirit! Blind to the Beauties of Art!"

"I'll never be an actress," I said. "And it's all my fault."

She sat down and took my hand. "It's not your fault," she said.

"No, I suppose not." I stared at the table and felt anger rising in my chest. "She has no right to stop me from being in the play. She's an awful woman, and I don't care what she thinks!"

"You could stay here until your parents return," suggested Isabelle.

I looked at her. "Stay here?" I said. "No. I couldn't do that."

"Why not? We have company all the time. You can sleep with Bets and me in the girls' bed."

"I shouldn't have run away," I said, my eyes filling with tears. "Everyone will be worried. They won't know what to think. They'll think I've been kidnapped and they'll come looking for me and I couldn't possibly bother your family and what if—"

"Are you hungry? We must fatten you up if you want to be on the stage," she said, rising. "Put some meat on your bones. When you walked in here, you looked like a drowned cat. *Meow*." She put up her hands like paws and scratched the air.

I managed to smile. "Meow," I said quietly.

"Then again, you do have the heart of a lion," she added, ruffling my hair. "*Rrrrr!*" she roared and pretended to pounce.

I laughed. Then I sighed. "I'm sorry," I said.

"For what?"

"For being such a bother."

"It's no bother. I know an artistic soul when I see one. It's no surprise that you ran away. It's only a wonder you put up with that woman for so long." She began to rummage in a cabinet.

She thinks I'm an artistic soul, I thought.

"I'm afraid there's not much to eat," she said.

"Isabelle?"

"Mmm?"

"Maybe I could join your troupe. Until Mama and Papa return?"

CHAPTER TWENTY-SIX

The Dance

She looked straight into my eyes. "I have just the part for you," she said.

"Then I can join? Mustn't you ask your mother?"

She shrugged. "We do what we like with the troupe."

As if on cue, Raymond wandered in, carrying an armful of notebooks. He dumped them on the table and sat down. He was wearing a loose, white gown that revealed his legs. I had never seen a man's legs before, not even Papa's. I stared at the floor.

"How are the new poems?" said Isabelle.

"Verily they are the exaltation of angels," said Raymond.

A petite, older woman walked in. "Mother, this is Penelope Bailey," said Isabelle. "Penelope, this is my mother, Mrs. Grey."

"How do you do?" I said.

"Lovely to meet you, dear," said Mrs. Grey in a breathy voice. "What beautiful red hair. Would you care for some breakfast—or is it lunch? Raymond does sleep late—what time is it? Ten?"

Mrs. Grey was thin and delicate, like a small bird. She fluttered to a window. "Look, the sky is clear," she said. "No more rain. Sunshine, puffy clouds—what is everyone planning? Hungry?" She opened a cabinet. "Oh dear," she said. She opened another cabinet. "Tsk. I forgot to do the marketing." She reached deep into the corner. "Look! Here are some of those apples we picked in October. If there's a saving grace to this freezing apartment, it's that the apples keep well—Raymond's favorite, aren't they dear? Plenty of apples."

Raymond rose and helped himself to several small, red apples. "Thank you, Mother. Mornin', Penelope," he said, tossing one to me and balancing another on his head.

Just then Artie and Bets tumbled into the kitchen, both talking at once. They greeted me with hugs and kisses. In the presence of all of them I felt suddenly shy.

Bets removed the apple from Raymond's head and looked at the table covered with notebooks. "What's all this?" she said, making a face.

"All what?" said Raymond. He pushed his arm across the table, and the notebooks fell to the floor. "New poems. Masterpieces," he said, winking at me.

I nibbled on my apple as Isabelle and her brothers began a heated conversation about the music for their next performance. Raymond wanted modern music—Ravel, I thought he said—but Artie wanted Bach. Isabelle held out for Beethoven. They argued for a while, their voices rising.

"Beethoven is majestic," said Isabelle. "Imagine 'Ode to Joy.'" She stood and started to dance around the table, singing in a loud voice.

"Too bombastic," shouted Raymond.

"No!" yelled Artie. "Bach! Bach!"

Isabelle waved her arms for silence. "Brothers," she said. "And sister. Now that you are all here, I have an announcement. The noble Penelope wants to join our troupe."

They all turned to look at me.

I could feel my face turning red. "Oh," I sputtered. "I shouldn't have presumed—"

"Nonsense," said Isabelle. "You are one of us. You are a leaf blown by the wind." She turned to her mother. "Penelope needs a place to stay," she said. "Her home circumstances being what they are—"

"Poor dear," said Mrs. Grey.

"What home circumstances?" said Bets.

"No, no," I said, waving my hands. "I don't want to trouble you. I spoke rashly before. I shouldn't have—"

"We certainly understand strained circumstances," said Mrs. Grey. "My children's friends are always welcome. Stay as long as you like."

Isabelle smiled at me. I bit my lip. The Greys were so welcoming, but if they couldn't pay the rent or the coal man, how could they afford to take me in? They didn't seem to have enough to eat, even for themselves.

"Now that you're here," said Isabelle, "we have three girls—you, me, and Bets. So you must stay, because I've a plan for three girls—a tableau from a Botticelli painting. We'll be 'The Three Graces.' I've already composed the dance in my mind. Ray, you must write a poem to go with it, and the music—Oh! No! Never mind, I have a splendid idea! In honor of Penelope, we'll rehearse on the beach today!"

"You can go to the beach in the winter?" I asked.

"Why not?" said Isabelle. "Does not Mother Ocean call to us in winter? Do her waves cease because it is cold? Of course not! They tumble with a force known only to those brave and hardy souls who dare venture forth, even in the face of adversity. Fishermen, merchantmen, mermen—"

"Actors," said Artie.

"Dancers," said Isabelle.

"Poets!" said Raymond, pounding his hand on the table.

"All right, all right," said Bets, rolling her eyes.

"It seems a lovely plan," said Mrs. Grey. "Unfortunately I can't join you. My first piano student comes at half past ten." She took down a round, metal tin from a high shelf and opened the top. "Here's something," she said, handing a nickel to Bets. "You can buy yourselves some bread on the way."

Artie jumped up and popped the nickel into his pocket. "Bread. The staff of life," he said. "Thank you, Mother!"

He picked up Isabelle and twirled her around, nearly knocking over Mrs. Grey. Isabelle squealed. I thought Mrs. Grey would tell them to calm down, but she didn't. Raymond pushed back his chair and shouted, "Unhand her, you brute!" while Isabelle yelled out, "To the ocean we must wend our way, the crashing waves summon us!" and Bets laughed and laughed.

I had never seen a family like this. They were so alive! I felt light-headed.

"Let's go!" said Isabelle.

"But Raymond isn't dressed yet," said Bets. "And you're still in your robe."

"Oh! I forgot," said Isabelle, looking down. Her blue Chinese robe rippled around her bare feet. "Everyone shall wear white! We assemble in the front hall!"

She grabbed my hand and pulled me to the bedroom. Slipping out of her robe, she donned a white crepe tunic, its wide sleeves edged in gold.

"Your clothes are still wet," she said. She flung open a wardrobe and began to throw clothing onto the bed. "Here, I've outgrown this, it should fit you," she said, tossing me a dress and some hose.

I took off my wet clothes and pulled on the dress. It was a fine ivory wool with a high waist, elaborately embroidered with tropical birds. The colors were slightly faded, but it must have cost a pretty penny when it was new.

In the front hall Mrs. Grey handed me my shoes and stockings, which had been somewhat dried by the fire in the stove, and Mama's shawl.

Isabelle wrapped a white silk shawl around her waist. "Everyone ready?" she said.

Raymond, Artie, and Bets nodded.

"Mother, we take our leave," said Isabelle.

"Ta-ta," said Mrs. Grey.

Isabelle charged out the door and we followed, tripping down the stairs to the street. I couldn't believe I was going to the beach. To rehearse! But when we came out of the dark staircase into the bright sunlight, I felt a pang of guilt.

I should be in school. Hunched over my Latin book, studying grammar. With Mr. Ducree.

I shook the thought out of my head. I was going to be an actress. I would bare my soul. What a wild thought! Hadn't Mr. Prenderwinkel said an actor should be wild?

The Greys chattered gaily as we made our way down the street. We stopped at a bakery and bought a loaf of bread, tearing off pieces and stuffing them into our mouths as we walked along. We boarded a cable car, then the Sutro railroad. The conductor looked surprised to see us. Aside from a fisherman or two, we were the only ones aboard.

At the end of the line, Isabelle jumped off the train. It was still moving, and the conductor yelled at her, but she wasn't listening. She dashed across the road and disappeared over the bluff. As soon as the train stopped, Raymond and Artie got off and ran after her, looking neither left nor right but barreling straight ahead with no thought as to whether a carriage might be coming. Bets and I hurried to catch up.

By the time we reached the bluff, Raymond and Artie were making their way down the slope. Isabelle was already at the water's edge, her shoes abandoned on the beach nearby. She stood there for a moment, not moving, alone on the broad beach except for the ocean and the sand and the pale winter sky. Then she started to dance, skipping and running and leaping over the sand.

Raymond and Artie were halfway to the water. Suddenly, Raymond stretched his arms out to his sides and began a dance of his own, spinning round and round in circles. Artie laughed. Bets and I caught up, and Artie whirled on us and started to tickle Bets. She screamed, threw some sand in his direction, and ran away. With a yell he took off after her.

I watched Isabelle dance. She waved her arms over her head, back and forth, back and forth, like seaweed floating on water. She bent low to the ground and spurted upward like a fountain. She flew across the sand with arms outstretched to the sky. She sank to the ground and wiggled her bare feet in the air.

I looked from Isabelle to Raymond, still spinning in his circles. Even though it was winter, neither of them wore a coat, and Raymond had nothing but sandals on his feet. I shivered and began rubbing my arms, which were covered with goose pimples. A fierce wind blew sand against my legs.

Isabelle skipped toward me. "Isn't it glorious?" she said, her eyes gleaming.

I could taste the salt in the air. "Aren't your feet cold?" I said.

She flopped onto the sand. I sat, too. The sand was still damp from the morning rain.

"Squint your eyes and look at the sand up close," she said, holding up a handful. "You think it's tan, but it isn't. Look! All the colors of the rainbow!" She threw the sand into the air and it blew down the beach.

I scooped up some sand and held it to my face. She was right. Up close I could see all the colors of the rainbow.

She lay down on her back and looked at the sky. For a few moments she didn't say anything. Then she spoke.

"You should stay with us forever."

Before I could answer, she was on her feet again, calling to Raymond. By now he, too, was lying sprawled on the sand. She skipped over to him, and I followed. He was muttering to himself.

"Ray," she said, giving him a little kick with her toe.

When he didn't answer, she walked away. Again I followed. She grasped my hand and ran toward the ocean, pulling me along behind her. As we approached the water, I pulled back. The waves were gigantic.

"Not so close!" I shouted, but the wind whipped the words out of my mouth and whisked them away before she could hear them.

She pulled me to the very edge of the water, then halted.

"Look!" she said.

A huge wave was about to crash. The blue-green water gathered strength like a lion about to pounce, then with a roar curled over on itself and came rushing toward us, its edge foaming white. Isabelle stepped forward to meet it.

"Isabelle!" I shouted.

She gripped my hand. I tried to pull away, but she wouldn't let go.

"Do you hear it?" she shouted.

"Hear what?"

"The heartbeat. The heartbeat of Mother Ocean."

The foaming water rushed toward us. "Isabelle!" I said. "Stop it!" I struggled to pull my hand free. "Let go!" I cried.

She laughed. I wrenched my hand free and jumped back. The water washed over Isabelle's feet.

"Aaaa! It's cold!" she said, still laughing. She scooped up a handful of the freezing water and tossed it at me.

"Stop it!" I said. "You scared me. Why did you do that?"

"Come in! Come in the water!" she said.

She began to dance again, stomping and splashing at the edge of the foam. She sang as she danced, lifting her knees high and flapping her arms like a bird. She unwound her shawl from about her waist and held it over her head like a sail. The white fringes of the shawl flapped around her face. Her dance was so astonishing, I forgot all about my anger.

If she catches the wind right, she might even be able to fly.
I wish I could dance like Isabelle.

I began to swing my arms. Isabelle nodded encouragement. She swooped her body sideways, and I swooped, too. She jumped high in the air. I jumped even higher.

"Brava!" she yelled.

She began to run down the beach, singing, her shawl trailing behind her. I held Mama's shawl above my head and chased her down the sand. I didn't know her song, so I sang one of my own. We ran and ran until we found ourselves at a little hollow beneath the bluff. There we collapsed in a heap, out of breath, laughing until the tears ran down our cheeks.

The wind was howling. We huddled close. A seagull circled above us, shrieking. It hung in midair, then dove for the water.

"Won't you stay forever, Princess Penelope?" said Isabelle. "Won't you stay and join our troupe of actors and dancers extraordinaire? Or will you return to the evil Aunt Phyllis and her evil daughters?" She laughed, then leaned into me with a serious look. "Do not betray your heart, Princess," she said.

I stopped laughing and wiped the tears from my cheeks. I dug my fingers into the sand. I wanted to say yes. I wanted to act and dance with Isabelle, to fly and leap across the earth, to feel the wind in my hair, to stand on a stage and make people laugh and weep, to hear the applause that was meant for me.

I looked into her wild eyes. I scooped up a handful of sand and let it fall through my fingers onto the end of Mama's shawl. Staring at the swirls of red and yellow and blue, I thought of Mama and I knew what my answer had to be.

"I can't," I said. "I can't stay forever. I have to go back."

"Why?"

"Because I'm not a leaf blown by the wind. I'm not an orphan. My parents love me, and I love them, and they're coming back for me. And even if Aunt Phyllis wouldn't let me be in the play, even if she is an awful woman . . ." I looked away. "She was only doing what she thought right."

"How could you put up with a woman like that?" said Isabelle.

"At least she's not my mother," I said, wiping my nose.

"Why don't you go home to Berkeley and wait for your parents there?" she said. "I'll come with you and we can live in the hills and dance in the woods, like Queen Titania and the forest creatures in *A Midsummer Night's Dream*." She stood and started to dance around me.

I shivered. "It's cold in the hills," I said. "And the ground is hard."

Isabelle stopped dancing. "Aunt Phyllis," she said. "She doesn't see what you are."

"What am I?" I said. "I'm nothing. I'm not an actress. I'm not even in the play." I put my head in my hands and began to cry. "I'll never be an actress. Not after what I've done. Mama will never let me take elocution lessons."

She put an arm around my shoulder.

"But you are," she said. "You are an actress. Acting has nothing to do with elocution. I act when I'm dancing, and I don't say a word. Acting is about one human heart speaking to another. And you already know how to do that."

She rose and turned to face me. Slowly her arms floated up from her sides. She placed her hands on her heart and closed her eyes. Then she lifted her arms above her head, opened them to the sky, and bowed to me. She swayed to one side, then another, and began a slow dance of such melancholy beauty that I didn't dare move. All the while she hummed a beautiful tune. The melody seemed unearthly, as if it came from another world. Where her dance came from and what it was called I do not know. I only know that as she danced I could scarcely breathe.

When she was done, she sank to the ground in a low bow. A feeling of peace came over me. I smiled at her.

"Oh, Isabelle," I said. "That was the most beautiful acting I've ever seen."

CHAPTER TWENTY-SEVEN

The Unexpected Guest

In the end we didn't rehearse at the beach. Isabelle said she wasn't in the mood, Raymond said the Muses weren't smiling on him, and Artie said his stomach was too empty. Bets said what kind of troupe are we, we'll never be a success if we don't rehearse. Then she stomped her foot and stalked off. I felt bad for Bets.

Hungry, tired, and chilled to the bone, we made our way back to Isabelle's. It must have been near five o'clock by the time we arrived. As we climbed the stairs to the apartment, I could hear Mrs. Grey playing the piano. The notes fluttered up and down, much like Mrs. Grey. We had just come through the door when the piece ended and someone in the parlor started to clap.

"Well done," said a man's voice. "Your students are fortunate indeed."

"You're very kind," said Mrs. Grey. "Another cup of tea while you wait? I'm sure the children will be back soon."

"We're home *now!*" yelled Isabelle, pulling me into the parlor.

"*How now, my headstrong, where have you been gadding?*" said the man.

"*Romeo and Juliet,*" said Isabelle. "Act Four."

"Right you are," he said, rising.

I was so stunned I couldn't say a word.

"Mr. Prenderwinkel, may I present my daughter, Isabelle,"

said Mrs. Grey. "Isabelle, this is Cornelius Prenderwinkel."

"*The* Cornelius Prenderwinkel?" asked Isabelle.

Mr. Prenderwinkel held out his hand. "A pleasure to meet you, Miss Grey," he said.

"The honor is mine, sir!" said Isabelle, pumping his hand vigorously.

"What are you doing here?" I blurted.

"Looking for you, of course."

"But who . . . how . . ."

"Where else but the Greys?" he said. "Dancers and Actors Extraordinaire." He winked at Isabelle.

"But how did you know I was missing?" I said, recovering my wits. "How did you find me? What made you look here? Does Aunt Phyllis know? What will happen now? Do you know the Greys?"

Mr. Prenderwinkel smiled. "The Greys were not of my acquaintance until today. But who better to harbor a soul like yours than fellow thespians?"

Isabelle beamed.

"Your cousin Aldebaran is an excellent detective," said Mr. Prenderwinkel.

"He is?" I said.

"Allow me to explain," he said. "The teachers sent Aldebaran home to see if you were there, but no one was home. Your aunt was out, the cook had gone to market, and the parlor maid had taken the day off to visit an ailing relative. Aldebaran came to my house, thinking you might have taken refuge there. When I got home at half past twelve, I found him sitting on my doorstep. Together we searched the house and garden, to no avail. We thought you might return of your own accord, but by two"—he held out his empty hands—"the jig was up. Your aunt had returned." He leaned forward. "I must say your disappearance threw the Leuts household into quite an uproar."

I bit my lip. I could picture Aunt Phyllis in an uproar.

"By half past two the police were contacted."

"Oh, no!"

"I wasn't too worried. I don't share your aunt's belief that San Francisco is full of depraved souls. Besides, you have a good head on your shoulders. Needless to say, the police commenced a search. Of course it never occurred to anyone to look for you at the beach. Very clever, Miss Grey," he said, turning to Isabelle.

"I wasn't hiding her," said Isabelle.

"Nevertheless," he said, "you succeeded in keeping the police—and Mrs. Leuts—off Penelope's trail."

By this time, Artie and Raymond and Bets had all crowded into the parlor to listen to Mr. Prenderwinkel's story.

"I accompanied young Aldebaran back to school to see if we could gather some clues to your whereabouts. Spoke with your teacher, Miss Adelaide. She introduced me to your friend. The bright-eyed one with the dark hair."

"Consuela," I said.

"Yes. She had filled in for you at the afternoon performance, and they were preparing for the evening."

I swallowed hard.

"Miss Adelaide and Consuela and Aldebaran and I asked each other, 'Where would Penelope go? Who does she know in San Francisco?' Your cousin thought of Isabelle, and Consuela said how much you admired her."

"Me?" said Isabelle. "She told them about me?"

"You are quite memorable, Izzy," said Artie.

Isabelle grinned. Then she frowned. "But must she go back? I have an idea for a tableau for three girls, based on Botticelli's 'The Three Graces,' and it requires—"

"Yes, I must," I said. "I must go back." I turned to Mr. Prenderwinkel. "But I still don't understand how you found the Greys."

"After our visit to your school, Aldebaran went home. It was nearly four o'clock. I hailed a cab and went to the California Theatre to make some inquiries. I thought someone there might know the Greys—theater people all seem to know each other, don't they?—and sure enough, our stage manager not only knew the Greys, he knew where they lived. So I made my way here, arriving not fifteen minutes ago. Mrs. Grey was kind enough to entertain me with her piano playing and a cup of Assam tea while I awaited your return." He smiled, pleased with his story.

"I'm sorry," I said quietly. "I didn't mean to cause trouble. Especially for you."

"Of course you are sorry," said Mr. Prenderwinkel, with a sympathetic smile. "Aldebaran said Mrs. Leuts had forbidden you to perform. Is that why you ran away?"

Tears welled up in my eyes. "Aunt Phyllis doesn't understand. She thinks I'm improper. But I'm not. I am an actress."

Mr. Prenderwinkel nodded.

"The principal was going to switch me to Mr. Ducree's class, so I ran away. I didn't know where I was going. I found Isabelle's card in my pocket,"—I looked at Isabelle—"and I thought of her dancing and her troupe and of what you said about actors."

"What did I say?" asked Mr. Prenderwinkel.

"You said an actor has to be wild. And so of course I thought of Isabelle."

Raymond snorted. "She's wild all right."

"And how," agreed Artie.

"Too wild sometimes," said Bets.

"Maybe a little," I said. I swallowed hard. "And . . . there was another reason I ran away."

"What was that?" asked Mr. Prenderwinkel.

"What if something happens to Mama and Papa? What if they drown on their way home and I have to stay with Aunt Phyllis and Uncle Henry forever? I couldn't bear . . . I couldn't bear the thought of . . . of . . ." I began to cry.

Isabelle put an arm around me. For a moment everyone was quiet.

I wiped my eyes. "I'm sorry to be such a bother."

"Will you come home now, my dear?" asked Mr. Prenderwinkel gently.

"I'll get my things."

"Your clothes are hanging in the kitchen," said Mrs. Grey. "They'll be dry by now."

Isabelle went with me to the kitchen. She watched as I gathered my belongings.

"You keep the dress," she said. "It suits you." She shook her head. "I wish we could do 'The Three Graces.'"

"Me, too," I said.

"You must visit, then. And in the meantime you must practice your dancing. I'll work on 'The Three Graces' and perhaps when you're older. . . . No, we won't wait till you're older. We cross the bay quite often and *I* will visit *you* in Berkeley."

"I would love that!" I said.

"And when I visit we will go to the hills and dance." Her eyes were shining. "Perhaps we will meet Queen Titania there, in the eucalyptus grove."

"I love the smell of eucalyptus."

"Me, too. And do you know something?"

I looked at her.

"Someday you *will* be an actress."

"Do you truly think so?"

"Of course."

I hugged her. We went back to the parlor, and I said my goodbyes. Then Isabelle handed me Mama's shawl, Mr. Prenderwinkel took my hand, and we made our way down the narrow stairs to the street.

CHAPTER TWENTY-EIGHT

The Homecoming

Mr. Prenderwinkel hailed a carriage, and we climbed aboard. The seat cushion was lumpy, and I couldn't get comfortable. All I could think about was what kind of punishment was in store for me. I pictured Aunt Phyllis locking me in the attic.

"Nervous?" said Mr. Prenderwinkel. "Or are you always a fidgety-wicket?"

"My aunt is going to punish me," I said.

"Now, now. I'm sure your aunt will be glad to see you. As for punishment, you'll bear up. You don't lack for courage."

"It wasn't very brave of me to run away. It was cowardly."

"No," he said. "Hasty, perhaps. A bit impetuous. But not cowardly." He bent his head toward my ear. "I suspect she drove you to it."

"Isabelle says Aunt Phyllis doesn't see me for what I am."

"It would be difficult for a woman of her background."

"Now I've lost everything. No *Romeo and Juliet*. No elocution lessons."

"Perhaps not everything," he said.

"I'll never be an actress now."

He thought for a moment. "Perhaps you could be a play-wright instead?"

I stared out the carriage window. "Girls don't write plays."

"Of course they do. Haven't you heard of Elizabeth Inchbald? Late eighteenth century? No? Or Eden Phillpotts? Her operetta, *Breezy Mornings*? How about Mrs. T. E. Smale? *The Compromising Case*. Haymarket Theatre, 1888."

"I don't want to be a playwright," I said. "I want to act."

"Hmm," said Mr. Prenderwinkel. "True enough." He stroked his chin. "Penelope?"

"Yes?"

"I didn't say an actor has to be wild."

"You didn't? I thought—"

"I said an actor has to be wild *and* disciplined. Without the discipline an artist never amounts to much."

The carriage pulled up in front of Aunt Phyllis's house. My legs felt heavy as we climbed the steps to the front door. Mr. Prenderwinkel lifted the dragon knocker and let it fall. I held my breath. The door swung open with a *whoosh*.

"Penny!" said Aldy, throwing his arms around me. "Where were you? Did you have an adventure? What a hubbub! Mother's been hysterical. Father called the police. Mother! Father! Penny's home!"

A tall policeman in a blue uniform appeared behind Aldy. "So this here's the little lady what's caused all the trouble," he said.

We entered the house. Violet and Petunia watched from the stairs as I hung Mama's shawl on a hook. Aunt Phyllis came rushing in, followed by Uncle Henry.

"Penelope!" she cried. Her voice was hoarse, her eyes puffy. "And you!" She stared at Mr. Prenderwinkel.

My stomach lurched. "I'm sorry," I said, lowering my gaze.

"Mrs. Leuts, Mr. Leuts," said Mr. Prenderwinkel, bowing slightly. "The steadfast Penelope is home from her wanderings."

There was a fat silence. I looked up. Aunt Phyllis's mouth hung open. She was speechless. I'd never seen her speechless.

"Glad you folks is reunited," said the policeman. "I'll call off the search."

"Thank you, Officer," said Uncle Henry, shaking the policeman's hand and showing him out the door.

Then Uncle Henry turned to Mr. Prenderwinkel. "Please, won't you come into the parlor? We are in your debt. I don't know how to thank—"

"It's quite all right," said Mr. Prenderwinkel.

"No, you must come in," said Uncle Henry, taking Aunt Phyllis's arm. "My dear?"

He walked her into the parlor, and we all followed. Aunt Phyllis looked wobbly. Uncle Henry helped her into a chair.

"Excuse me," she said, wiping her eyes. "I am quite overcome."

"There, there," said Mr. Prenderwinkel. He took a handkerchief from his pocket and held it out. "Everything's all right now, Mrs. Leuts. She's back. No harm done."

She took the handkerchief but didn't look at him. "Penelope, how could you do such a thing? We were worried sick." She turned her gaze to Mr. Prenderwinkel. "How on earth did *you* find her? How did you know where to look when the police—"

"My dear madam," said Mr. Prenderwinkel. "I simply used my powers of deduction. We actors are more intelligent than we're generally given credit for."

"But a mere vaudevillian—"

"Now, dear," said Uncle Henry. "I'm sure Mr. Prenderwinkel is more than a mere vaudevillian. He is a Shakespearean actor, I believe." He smiled at Mr. Prenderwinkel. "And we have him to thank for Penny's return."

Aunt Phyllis looked Mr. Prenderwinkel up and down. "Well," she said, sniffing. "If you say so." She dabbed her eyes with Mr. Prenderwinkel's handkerchief. "Thank you," she said.

It was my turn to be speechless. I never thought I'd see Aunt

Phyllis thanking Mr. Prenderwinkel for anything.

Mr. Prenderwinkel turned and motioned for me to come closer to Aunt Phyllis. I approached and sank to my knees.

"Please forgive me, Aunt Phyllis," I said, bowing my head.

For a moment no one said a word. Aunt Phyllis straightened her skirts.

"What do you say, dear?" said Uncle Henry.

"The quality of mercy is not strained; It droppeth as the gentle rain from heaven," said Mr. Prenderwinkel.

"Amen," said Uncle Henry.

Aunt Phyllis looked at Mr. Prenderwinkel in astonishment. "What did you say? Forgive me. I am not accustomed to hearing actors quote the Bible."

Mr. Prenderwinkel smiled. "I'm sorry to disappoint you, Mrs. Leuts," he said, "but it's not the Bible. It's Shakespeare. *The Merchant of Venice.*"

Aunt Phyllis took a sharp little breath.

"Perhaps you'd like to see it sometime," said Mr. Prenderwinkel. "I'd be happy to arrange for front row seats the next time it's in town."

Aunt Phyllis blanched.

"That's very generous," said Uncle Henry.

"Yes, well, ahem," said Aunt Phyllis. She shifted in her seat and looked at Uncle Henry.

Mr. Prenderwinkel bowed slightly. "Mrs. Leuts, Mr. Leuts, please excuse me. I must be going."

"Indeed," said Aunt Phyllis. She sounded relieved.

"Hope to see you folks at the theater sometime," said Mr. Prenderwinkel.

"A-choo!" Aunt Phyllis sneezed.

"God bless you," said Mr. Prenderwinkel.

"Thank you," said Aunt Phyllis, holding the handkerchief

to her nose with one hand and waving the other hand in the air as if to shoo him away.

"I'll see you to the door," said Uncle Henry, leading him out. "Tell me, what play are you rehearsing?"

"*The Tempest*," said Mr. Prenderwinkel. "California Theatre, five performances a week. Every day save Thursday and Sunday."

Their voices faded. Aunt Phyllis fanned herself with the handkerchief. The color returned to her cheeks.

"Penelope, get off your knees," she said. "Where did you get that gaudy dress?"

"From my friend," I said, standing up.

"We have some serious talking to do, young lady, but first I must compose myself. Violet, Petunia, Aldebaran, go finish your supper."

Violet and Petunia hadn't said a word since I entered the house. Now Petunia piped up.

"Mother?"

"Just a moment," said Aunt Phyllis, blowing her nose.

Aldy took a dinner roll out of his pocket and popped it into his mouth.

"Excuse me, Mother?" said Petunia.

"Yes?" said Aunt Phyllis.

"May I please go to school tonight? Would you mind? I've been asked to play the violin for Miss Adelaide's class performance."

CHAPTER TWENTY-NINE

Petunia's Request

There was a thud as Aunt Phyllis fell back against her chair. "What on earth are you talking about?" she said.

"The music teacher at school is friends with Professor Entwhistle, my teacher at the conservatory," said Petunia. "They both thought it would be nice if I played my violin in between the scenes of the play."

"Nice?" Aunt Phyllis looked like she was going to explode. She leaned forward. "How long have you known about this? And when was I to be informed?" Her eyes were near to popping out of her head.

"I know, I know," said Petunia, holding up her hand. "I should've told you earlier."

"Darn tootin'," said Aldy, under his breath.

Aunt Phyllis whipped her head in my direction. "Did you know about this?" She was pressing her fingers so hard into the arms of the chair that they left little dents in the fabric.

I shook my head.

"Father, may I play my violin at the school performance?" said Petunia to Uncle Henry, who had just walked in.

"Ask your mother, my pet," said Uncle Henry. "What school performance?"

"Tonight," said Petunia. "Miss Adelaide's class is performing

Selected Scenes and Sonnets from Shakespeare, and—"

"Oh, ho," said Uncle Henry.

"We can hardly allow you to perform in public when Penelope is forbidden to do so," said Aunt Phyllis.

"But Professor Entwhistle said it would be a good experience," said Petunia.

"No buts!" said Aunt Phyllis.

"But I already played for the afternoon performance."

Uncle Henry raised his eyebrows. I looked at Aldy. He raised his eyebrows, too.

Aunt Phyllis turned red. "Already played—"

"Miss Tumleigh picked me 'specially to play the music. Just me. No one else. Professor Entwhistle thinks I'm very talented. Don't you think I'm talented?"

"Of course you're talented!" said Aunt Phyllis.

"Talent should not go to waste," said Petunia. "That's what you always said."

"Hmph," said Aunt Phyllis. She rose and began to pace about the room.

"Waste not, want not," said Petunia. "You said that, too. Didn't she, Father?"

"Indeed she did," said Uncle Henry.

All eyes were on Aunt Phyllis as she circled the table. "Will Professor Entwhistle be there?" she said.

"Yes," said Petunia. "And Mrs. Stanford, too. Her nephew's in the play."

Aunt Phyllis froze in her tracks. "*The* Mrs. Stanford?"

Petunia nodded.

"Her nephew? In Miss Adelaide's play? What's his name?"

"Horace something," said Petunia.

"Figures," said Aldy.

Aunt Phyllis whirled around. "Fine," she snapped. "You may play. We will go. Penelope, too." She narrowed her eyes at me.

"But *you* will not perform. I have not changed my opinion of the theater. You may watch someone else's child make a spectacle of herself as an actress."

"That would be Consuela Hop-skins," said Petunia. "The understudy."

"Hopkins," said Violet.

"Can we eat now?" said Aldy.

Aunt Phyllis ignored him. "Henry, please excuse me, I must freshen up. Aldy and Petunia, be ready in ten minutes. Penelope, we will deal with your transgressions tomorrow." She strode toward the door.

"What about me?" said Violet.

"What about you?" said Aunt Phyllis. "You are not going anywhere. You are a tattler. Go to your room."

Violet looked fit to be tied. She stomped off.

"Is anyone hungry?" said Aldy. "I'm going to finish my mashed potatoes and stew."

"Penelope?" said Uncle Henry.

"No, thank you," I said. My head was spinning.

"Pretty dress," said Uncle Henry.

Night had fallen by the time we set out for school. Petunia chattered all the way, but I didn't say a word. My brains had turned to mush, and it was all I could do to keep from falling over. Above all loomed one giant question: Why was Aunt Phyllis letting Petunia perform, when she wouldn't let me?

Aldy walked by my side. He could tell I was under a cloud.

"Mother wants to show her off," he said, as if he could read my mind. "She wants to impress Mrs. Stanford."

"I don't understand her," I said. "She said girls should be modest."

He shrugged. "Mrs. Stanford is rich," he said. He picked up the end of Mama's shawl, which had fallen off my shoulders, and handed it to me. "You would've made a good Juliet."

I pulled the shawl tight around me.

We joined the crowd pushing through the school doors. Aunt Phyllis waved to Mrs. Stanford. Mrs. Stanford barely nodded. Aunt Phyllis started complaining to Uncle Henry, saying Mrs. Stanford didn't have to be so uppity just because her husband was the richest man in the city.

We found some seats and waited for the performance to begin. I was so miserable I couldn't sit still, so I asked Aunt Phyllis if I could go to the bathroom, and she said yes.

I made my way up the crowded aisle. Petunia was standing in the hallway, surrounded by friends, clutching her violin case. She looked triumphant.

"Too bad you can't be in the play," she sneered.

Her friends stared. I turned and ran toward the ladies room, my face burning.

"I hope you enjoy my violin playing!" she called after me.

I slammed the door of the stall.

I wish I were dead, I thought, kicking the stall.

Hot tears spilled down my face. I sobbed, gulping for breath. *I don't want to be dead. I want to be an actress.*

Why can't Aunt Phyllis understand? Doesn't she have any feelings? Feelings are everything.

I wiped my eyes and stared at the cold tile floor.

Mama and Papa would understand. They would know what it meant to be friends with Mr. Prenderwinkel and to dance at the beach with Isabelle, with the wind howling and the ocean roaring and my heart leaping.

Suddenly I knew there was only one way I could ever make Aunt Phyllis understand. She had to see me act.

CHAPTER THIRTY

The Switch

I walked out of the bathroom, but instead of returning to the auditorium, I went to Miss Adelaide's room.

I peeked in the door. Miss Adelaide was standing by the window, straightening Linden's tie. Consuela sat alone near the door, brushing her hair.

"Psst! Consuela."

She turned around, and her jaw dropped open. I put a finger to my lips. She stood and edged toward the door.

"What are you doing here?" she said, slipping into the hall.

"Mr. Prenderwinkel found me at Isabelle's," I whispered.

"Are you in trouble?"

"Big trouble," I said.

"How did you get here?"

"When Aunt Phyllis found out Petunia had been invited to play the violin, she decided we should all come. She couldn't resist the chance to show her off. But she still won't let me act."

Consuela looked crestfallen. "Then what are you doing here?" she said.

"I came to . . . to ask you a favor." My heart skipped a beat. "Do you think . . . What would you think if . . . if I went on tonight?"

She gasped. "I thought you were in big trouble."

"It doesn't matter anymore. What else can she do to me? It's just that . . ." I shook my head. "No. I can't. I couldn't. It wouldn't be fair to you."

"Of course you can," she said. "I already had a turn at the afternoon performance. I'm only sorry you missed it."

"I'm sorry, too," I said. "I bet you were good."

"I didn't forget any lines," she said. She leaned close to whisper in my ear. "Even in the kiss parts."

The kiss parts. I took a deep breath. "I'm taking the stage," I said.

Consuela's eyes got very big.

"Don't say anything to Miss Adelaide. I don't want to get her into any more hot water."

"I won't," she said, putting a finger to her lips. She stepped back and looked me up and down. "You look like Juliet in that dress."

I smiled. "It's Isabelle's," I whispered.

It was almost time for the play to begin. Children began spilling out of the classroom into the hall. I snuck around a corner and hid. As Miss Adelaide's class filed into the auditorium and took seats in the first row, I slipped into the back and stood in the shadows. I could see Aunt Phyllis craning her neck, looking for me.

The auditorium was full to overflowing and looked very festive. Someone had hung red crepe paper flowers across the front of the stage. As if from far away, I heard the murmur of excited children and saw all the proud parents. I was so nervous I could scarcely breathe.

Miss Tumleigh stepped to the front, and everyone quieted down. She announced that there was a change in the program and that the part of Juliet would be played by Consuela Hopkins. Then the performance began.

The sonnet people went first. Aunt Phyllis kept shifting in

her seat. From time to time she turned around. I stayed in the shadows, and she didn't see me. Linden was fidgety, too. He must've been nervous, but he couldn't have been as nervous as me. My stomach was turning tumblesaults.

After the sonnets Petunia played the violin. Her tune had lots of fancy notes, which she played without mistakes, but without much feeling, either. Still, her playing was well received by the audience, and Aunt Phyllis, full of pride, looked all puffed-up in her seat. She kept turning around to see Mrs. Stanford's reaction. Mrs. Stanford clapped politely.

Then came the opening scenes of *Romeo and Juliet*—the "Prologue" and "The Slaying of Benvolio and Tybalt." The boys boomed their lines and seemed to be having a jolly time, especially with their wooden swords. Horace moved a bit stiffly, but at least he didn't sound stupid.

Just before our scene, the boys put out the platform that was our balcony. There was a rustle of programs as Linden rose. I felt a fluttering in my stomach and strode out of the shadows and down the aisle toward the stage. As I passed Consuela, she whispered, "Break a leg."

I lifted the hem of my skirt and stepped onto the platform. I heard Aunt Phyllis gasp. A sea of faces stared up at me. I didn't look at them but stared at the back of the room, as Miss Adelaide had instructed during rehearsal. Linden looked at me in surprise. He hesitated. His cheeks were flushed, and he looked very handsome.

"Go ahead," I whispered.

"*He jests at scars that never felt a wound,*" he said. "*But, soft! what light through yonder window breaks?*"

"*Ah me!*" I said.

"*She speaks,*" said Linden.

I had never felt anything like the feeling that came over me then, with all those eyes upon me and Shakespeare's words coming out of my mouth. The whole room was different somehow, like the air had changed. It was as if a light was shining down on me from heaven. All the work of the previous weeks disappeared and I felt like I was being carried away on a cloud, like in a dream. But I wasn't asleep. I was more awake than I'd ever been in my life.

And so it was that I kept right on going when we reached the second kiss part, and Linden leaned over and actually kissed me on the cheek! A murmur ran through the audience. I must have blushed beet red, for I could feel my cheeks grow hot. But I didn't falter in my lines. Instead I lifted my chin, threw the end of Mama's shawl over one shoulder, and carried on with even deeper feeling.

When we were finished, the applause started out small, then began to build. It swelled and swelled until it poured over us like rain on a hot day. People were standing and clapping. Someone shouted, "Bravo! Bravo!" We had to bow at least five times. Then Linden took my hand and helped me down from the platform. Everyone rushed forward to congratulate us, and suddenly we were caught in a swirl of people.

Miss Adelaide was the first to greet me. "Where did you come from? We were so worried! Are you all right? You were wonderful! You took my breath away." She put a hand on my shoulder and turned me around. "What a stunning dress. What exquisite embroidery. I love the colors in your shawl."

"Thank you," I said shyly.

"Miss Adelaide!" someone called.

"It's my mother's shawl," I said.

"Well, it's lovely," she said. She smiled and excused herself.

"Speaking of mothers. . . ," said Uncle Henry, coming up to us.

I turned around. Aunt Phyllis was striding down the aisle. Her eyes were glittering. I wanted to escape, but there was no place to go. She bore down on me like a ship with all her sails unfurled, and I thought to myself, I'd rather walk a gangplank for a pirate king than hear what Aunt Phyllis has to say.

I looked at the floor and waited for her to speak. When she didn't say anything, I looked up. She leaned towards me.

"You are a disobedient child," she said in a hoarse voice. "I am—"

"Phyllis," said Uncle Henry, "why don't you tell Penelope what you thought of her acting?"

Aunt Phyllis cleared her throat. "You were . . ." Her eyes flickered away from me. "It was . . . touching."

Uncle Henry grinned.

"Thank you," I said. Then a waving hand caught my eye. I looked up the other aisle, and I couldn't believe what I saw. Aldy was pushing through the crowd, with Mama and Papa close behind.

CHAPTER THIRTY-ONE

"All's Well That Ends Well"

Papa swept me up in his arms. "Splendid!" he said. "Simply splendid!"

Then Mama embraced me. Her perfume made her smell like a tropical flower. "You were wonderful, sweetie," she said, her eyes shining. "We are so proud of you." She looked beautiful, and not a bit tired from her long voyage.

"Mama," I said. "Mama." I held her tight and burst into tears.

"I'm right here, sweetheart," said Mama, wrapping me in her arms.

"Now, now, what's all the fuss, little butterfly?" said Papa.

"Papa!" I said, reaching out. "I missed you so much."

"There, there," said Papa.

"Don't you ever go away again," I sobbed.

"You don't have to worry about that," he said. "The university won't give me another sabbatical for seven years. By then you'll be quite the young lady."

"I believe she's quite the young lady now," said Mr. Prenderwinkel.

"You're here!" I said, letting go of Mama.

"I am," said Mr. Prenderwinkel.

I wiped the tears from my face and introduced Mr. Prenderwinkel to Mama and Papa. They Shook hands all around.

"Mr. Prenderwinkel is an actor," I said proudly.

Aunt Phyllis was standing a little ways off, with Petunia's hand firmly in her grasp. Her lips were twitching. When she caught my eye she started to speak. "If it were up to me—" she said.

"Penelope certainly is full of surprises, isn't she?" said Uncle Henry, interrupting. He banged Papa on the back. "Quite a gal you've got there, Ernest, quite a gal."

"Henry," said Aunt Phyllis.

Uncle Henry looked at her. "I think we should allow Penelope some time with her parents, don't you?" he said.

"Right you are," said Mr. Prenderwinkel. "I'll be taking my leave, then. Delighted to meet you, Mr. and Mrs. Bailey. Your daughter is quite a pip. Penelope, come and see me in *The Tempest*, won't you?"

"*The Tempest*?" said Papa. "Where's it playing?"

Aunt Phyllis's hand flew up to her mouth.

"California Theatre," said Mr. Prenderwinkel.

"Splendid!" said Papa. "We'll come. Once we've settled in at home. Crossing the bay is not nearly so daunting now that we've crossed the Pacific, is it dear?"

"No," said Mama. "It's not."

"Well then, I hope to have the pleasure of seeing you again soon," said Mr. Prenderwinkel. "And please come backstage after the performance." He bowed slightly.

Uncle Henry held out an arm for Aunt Phyllis. "Shall we go?" he said.

"By the way, Mrs. Leuts, your daughter is quite a fiddler," said Mr. Prenderwinkel, smiling at Petunia. "She does you credit."

Aunt Phyllis opened her mouth as if to speak, but nothing came out.

Petunia lifted her violin case. "Thank you, Mr. Prenderwinkel," she said. She glanced at Aunt Phyllis. "My mother is always encouraging me to play."

"Her encouragement has certainly paid off," he said.

Aunt Phyllis turned red. But I thought I saw a flicker of a smile cross her lips.

"Ah, there's Professor Entwhistle," said Uncle Henry, spying Petunia's violin teacher. "Come, dear." He took Aunt Phyllis's arm and led her away.

Aldy came rushing up. "Mr. Prenderwinkel! Would you come meet some of my friends?"

"By all means," said Mr. Prenderwinkel, and he and Aldy walked up the aisle toward a group of boys.

Again I threw my arms around Mama. "I didn't think you'd be here till Christmas!"

"Neptune smiled upon us," said Papa. "Favorable trade winds."

"But how did you know to come here?"

"We arrived at Aunt Phyllis' and Uncle Henry's just after you left. Mrs. Campbell told us where you were and gave us directions."

"We couldn't wait a moment longer to see you," said Mama.

I hugged her. "You didn't drown," I murmured.

"Drown?" said Mama.

"I was so afraid your ship would sink, or you'd be attacked by pirates, or a typhoon would come and blow you off course." My heart was full to bursting. "I'm so glad you're home!"

Mama smiled. "No, sweetie, we didn't drown," she said. "And it's wonderful to be home. But I'm sorry you gave Aunt Phyllis and Uncle Henry such a scare. Mrs. Campbell was telling me about it. It's quite unlike you to run off like that."

She lifted my chin and studied my face. I could see the disappointment in her eyes. I looked away, ashamed.

"Don't be angry," I said. "Please, Mama."

"Is Aunt Phyllis so terrible?"

"I tried to be good. Truly I did."

Mama and Papa looked at each other.

"Phyllis can be quite rigid," said Papa.

"Mmm," said Mama.

"Then why did you leave me with her?" I said.

They were silent for a moment. Then Mama said, "We had to, sweetie. Papa needed my help. Aunt Phyllis can be difficult, but she's family. I knew she'd take good care of you, and I was confident that even she couldn't ruin your lively spirit."

"Do you forgive me for running away? When are we going home?"

"Soon," said Mama. "Tomorrow. Papa's specimens are still being unloaded at the dock."

"I can't wait to go home," I said. "I miss Berkeley, and my friends, and school, and . . ." I hesitated.

"And?" said Mama and Papa together.

"Will you still let me take elocution lessons?"

A little smile crept across Papa's face.

"Running away is a serious infraction," said Mama. "And forging Aunt Phyllis's signature is worse. I think elocution lessons will have to wait."

"Oh," I said, my chin quivering.

"Where did you get that dress?" said Mama.

Just then Consuela came up to us with her parents.

"My parents are home!" I said.

Her face lit up. We introduced the parents. They started to chat as they walked up the aisle.

"What did you think?" I said to Consuela.

"You were great," she said. "You were as good as Sarah Bernhardt."

"She was, wasn't she?" said Aldy, joining us. "Can I walk home with you?"

I felt a rush of happiness.

It was quieter in the auditorium now. The last few stragglers were gathering their belongings and the janitor was starting to sweep the stage. Consuela said goodnight and left. Aldy and I drifted up the aisle.

Suddenly he poked me in the ribs. He was grinning from ear to ear. "Surprised you with that kiss, didn't he?" he said.

"He wasn't supposed to kiss me!" I said.

"Sure he was," said Aldy, poking me again.

I hit him on the arm, and he laughed. Then I laughed, too. We couldn't stop laughing.

I looked up to see Mr. Prenderwinkel talking with Mama and Papa at the back of the auditorium.

"And a promising actress she is, too," Mr. Prenderwinkel was saying.

"Mr. Prenderwinkel," I said, "why aren't you at the California Theatre? Don't you have your own performance tonight?"

"Five nights a week, save Thursday and Sunday," he said. "And today is Thursday."

"It was very nice of you to come," said Mama. "And on your night off."

"Not at all," said Mr. Prenderwinkel. "I stopped by the Leuts's house to retrieve my hat, and Mrs. Campbell told me you were here." He smiled at me and crinkled his eyes. "An auspicious debut, my dear. Perhaps someday I will let you have a small part in one of my plays."

My mouth fell open.

"The best way to learn, if you're going to be an actress, is to apprentice yourself in a real production."

Mama and Papa looked at each other. I didn't dare blink.

"Well," Mama said. "I suppose it can't be stopped."

"Yes," said Papa. "'It's a force of nature.'"

"A whirlwind," said Mama.

"Does that mean you would let me?" I said.

"You take after your mother, my sweet," said Papa. "It must run in the blood. Once an actress, always an actress."

"What do you mean?" I said.

"Why, just this, that when I met your mother, she was quite the actress herself. It's only in recent years that she's turned her artistry to painting and drawing."

I looked at Mama. "You were?" I said in astonishment.

Mama blushed. "Only an amateur actress," she said.

"And a more lovely one never graced the stage, I'm sure," said Mr. Prenderwinkel.

"You were an actress?" asked Aldy.

"A very proper actress," said Papa. "But don't go telling your mother."

It was Aldy's turn to gape.

I stared at Mama. Somehow she looked different. Taller and more beautiful than I had ever seen her before.

"Aldebaran, my boy, just because you're named after a star doesn't mean you're the only star in the family," said Mr. Prenderwinkel.

"I always wished you had named me after a star," I said to Mama and Papa, taking their hands in mine.

"You've always been our star," said Mama.

"The brightest one in all the heavens," said Papa.

I pulled them close. "And now I'll have my chance to shine," I said. And I smiled and led them outside, into the moonlit night.

Author's Note

In the second half of the nineteenth century, San Francisco was a brash, young city. As a result of the California gold rush and the completion of the transcontinental railroad, what had been a sleepy outpost of 850 people in 1848 had become by 1890 a bustling metropolis of 298,997 people.

During this period of rapid growth, San Franciscans were eager to embrace new technology. By 1889, when this story takes place, many stores and businesses already had telephones, and some even had electricity. (San Francisco was the first city in the world to have a central generating station for electricity, even before New York City and London.)

For San Francisco, as for the nation as a whole, the second half of the nineteenth century was a time of tremendous social change, too. Workers were beginning to ask for better working conditions, and women were demanding the right to vote and speaking out for dress reform. In fact, the effort of women to free themselves from the restrictions of the corset was one of the leading issues of the day.

Conflicting social forces also played out in the way that Americans viewed the theater. Ever since the Puritan days, some Americans had considered theater and dance sinful, and though by the nineteenth century there were theaters in every major city, a respectable middle-class girl of the time would have been strongly discouraged from considering any career outside the home, much less one in the theater. Still, by the late nineteenth century, San Franciscans were flocking to variety acts and vaudeville shows, as well as more traditional fare, like Shakespeare's plays. The 1,600-seat California Theatre on Bush Street, which opened in 1869, was one of approximately forty theaters in the city.

The inspiration for this book began with a woman who was born in San Francisco in 1877. Isadora Duncan (1877-1927) was the youngest of the four children of Mary Dora Gray and Joseph Charles Duncan. Isadora's parents divorced when she was very young, and because her father's financial support was spotty at best, Isadora's mother supported the family as best she could by giving piano lessons and selling the scarves, hats, and mittens that she knitted at home. Isadora grew up to become a great dancer, famous in both the United States and Europe for revolutionizing the art of dance and bringing it into the modern age. The character of Isabelle Grey is based on Isadora Duncan.

As a young person I dreamed of a life in the theater and was inspired by the writings of Isadora Duncan in much the same way that Penelope Bailey is inspired by Isabelle Grey. By creating a fictional character, I was able to make some changes in order to accommodate the needs of the story. For example, in 1889, the real Isadora Duncan was twelve, and her family had already moved across the bay to Oakland. Although I changed some historical details, I tried to capture something of the spirit of Isadora Duncan and her times, particularly the struggle between conventional middle-class expectations of girls and the romantic and rebellious impulses that led women like Isadora to foment change.

A Note About Sources

Many years ago I choreographed a dance based on Nathaniel Hawthorne's *The Scarlet Letter*. In the process of doing research for the dance, I read a great deal of nineteenth-century American literature, especially the novels of Hawthorne and the poetry of Emily Dickinson. When I began work on *Penelope Bailey Takes the Stage*, I wanted to get the sound of nineteenth-century American language into my ears again, and so I read and reread a number of novels from the period, including Louisa May Alcott's *Little Women*, Herman Melville's *Moby Dick*, Stephen Crane's *The Red Badge of Courage*, Mark Twain's *Huckleberry Finn*, and Edith Wharton's *Ethan Frome*.

Nonfiction books proved useful, as well, including *My Life, the autobiography of Isadora Duncan* (New York: Boni & Liveright, 1927); Peter Kurth's *Isadora: A Sensational Life* (Boston: Little, Brown, 2001); *Everyday Life in the Age of Enterprise, 1865-1900*, by Robert H. Walker (New York: Putnam, 1967); *Historic Spots in California*, by Mildred Brooke Hoover, Hero Eugene Rensch, and Ethel Grace Rensch (Stanford, CA: Stanford University Press, 3rd ed., rev. by William N. Abeloe, 1965); *The Victorian Home: The Grandeur and Comfort of the Victorian Era, in Households Past and Present*, by Ellen M. Plante (Philadelphia: Running Press, 1995); and

The American Heritage History of the Confident Years, by Francis Russell (New York: American Heritage/Bonanza Books, 1987).

The World Wide Web provided a wealth of information about life in nineteenth-century San Francisco, including such gems as a historic map of the city from 1873, and the entire contents of the San Francisco telephone directory of 1878. Two especially useful sites were those of the San Francisco Historical Society, www.sfhistory.org, and the Virtual Museum of the City of San Francisco, www.sfmuseum.org.